# Forty STEPS
## and Other Stories

TERRENCE MURPHY

# FORTY STEPS AND OTHER STORIES

iUniverse books may be ordered through booksellers or by contacting:

iUniverse
1663 Liberty Drive
Bloomington, IN 47403
www.iuniverse.com
1-800-Authors (1-800-288-4677)

ISBN: 978-1-5320-5301-6 (sc)
ISBN: 978-1-5320-5303-0 (hc)
ISBN: 978-1-5320-5302-3 (e)

Library of Congress Control Number: 2018908390

Print information available on the last page.

iUniverse rev. date: 07/27/2018

To Calantha Sears, curator emerita of the Nahant Historical Society

# $C$ONTENTS

# ᴀUTHOR NOTE

*Forty Steps and Other Stories* is a collection of sixteen tales set in Egg Rock, a fictional seaside town on the North Shore outside of Boston. The stories are arranged in approximate chronological order—with occasional flashbacks and glimpses of the future—between the years 1090 and 2110. Besides the setting, the stories are connected by the reappearance of characters and their ancestors or descendants. Some people who appear will be familiar to those who have read my novel *Assumption City*.

Many of the pieces are based on historical events or legends from the North Shore, but they are fictional renderings, not historical accounts. Each story can stand alone, but when read in order, the tales become more and more connected.

I was brought up on the North Shore, and although I have spent most of my life elsewhere, I have always loved that part of the world best of all. I hope these stories help the reader understand why.

# $\mathcal{A}$CKNOWLEDGMENTS

Without the help of those who shared their expertise and life experiences with me, this book would not have been possible.

My wife, Betty Wood Murphy, read these stories at every stage of development, offering invaluable advice and unflagging encouragement.

Jan Schreiber and Frederic E. Oder helped me make every story better than it might have been.

Much appreciated help came from Gerard Butler, Molly and Dave Conlin, Philip Crotty, Bonnie Ayers D'Orlando, James Harshbarger, Sharon Hawkes, Catherine Hutchison, Jim Littleton, Laura McPhee, Veronica N. Nanagas-Devon, Annapurna Poduri, Nancy Shea, Andre Sigourney, Rev. Frank Silva, Gretchen Sterenberg, and James Wood.

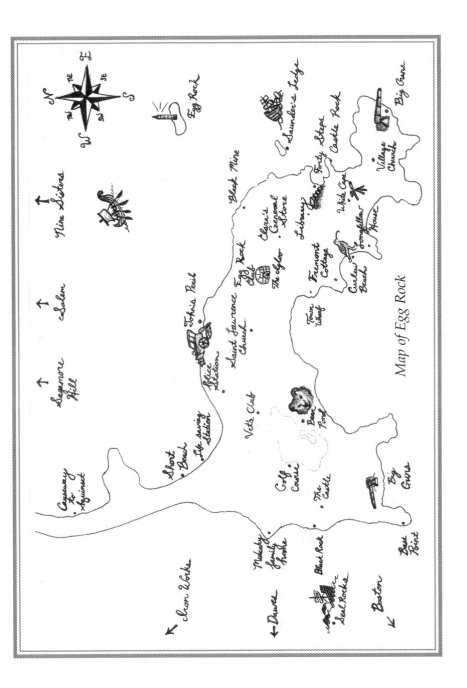

Map of Egg Rock

# $\mathcal{T}$HORVALD PAYS HIS RESPECTS

My name is Ragnhild. The word means "Battle Adviser," and as it suggests, I have been more of a thinker and talker than a warrior. The warrior's job is for more able men. I have spent much of my life on the sea, where I have witnessed my share of battles, bloodshed, courage, and despair. I left home at  fifteen and signed on as a rower of a Viking longship, with voyages to Denmark, islands known now as the Orkneys, and the north of England.

I can close my eyes and see myself—a bashful, blond, sunburned country boy still growing into my outsize hands and feet—seated in the longship for the first time. The great square sail towered over me, and a huge man old enough to be my father wrapped his gnarled fingers around the long steering oar to the starboard.

As thrilling as those experiences were, they were nothing compared to being chosen as an adviser to Thorvald Eiriksson, son of Erik the Red and brother of Leif, on his voyages to Vinland. Those days are long past, and I am now back in my village near Bergen, where I tend my little garden during the short but intense summer and warm my feet by the fire during our long winter nights. Thankfully, I'm close enough to the shore to smell the sea, hear the waves crash against the cliffs, and watch the seabirds whirl about in the breeze.

But my eyes are failing now, so most nights are given over to fitful sleep filled with vivid dreams of what I've seen and imagined— and fear. The outsize hands of my youth are crippled and painful, and I am but a bag of bones.

Thorvald chose me, he said, for my unusual feats of memory. Over campfires, he'd hear me tell story after story filled with the minutest detail long into the night. If questioned, I could describe the appearance of a casual acquaintance in astounding detail.

Pointing to my head, he once asked, "How can you fit all those memories inside?"

My assignment was not only to advise him on military matters but to remember everything. Someday in the future, sailors will be able to make notes as events unfold, but there was no way we could do such a thing in a longboat packed with thirty men and hardly enough room to stretch our legs.

While I'm still able, I am writing down as much detail of our Vinland voyages as possible because once I've departed earth and sit before Odin himself, there will be no one left to tell the story of Thorvald's last days.

We had just spent the third winter as far south as we'd ever ventured, on a large island where barely any snow fell, the ponds never iced over, and no natives appeared to disturb us. Once we broke camp in the spring and began our trip north, we approached a long, narrow land enclosing a large bay. We called that land

Kiarlarnes on account of its resemblance to a ship's keel. It was made up of grass-covered headlands punctuated by enormous sand dunes. What a desolate place!

We worked our way north, keeping the coastline in view on the western horizon. Late on our third day, we came upon a promontory covered with a wood, brilliant green in the spring sunshine.

Just as we put our oars down to savor the tranquil scene, a squall line sped toward us from the northwest. The sky darkened, the wind rose, and we were pelted with rain.

The youngest and least seasoned of our rowers, a boy named Sveinn, hadn't secured his oar correctly into its notch, and it flew off the hull into the water. He stood and reached for it, when a large wave nearly capsized the boat, and swept him overboard. It all happened in an instant. The squall passed as suddenly as it had arrived. The sun came out, and the sea calmed. The errant oar floated in calm waters a boat's width away, as if nothing important had taken place.

But there was no sign of the boy.

The boats crisscrossed—seemingly hundreds of times—the place where he'd gone down. We all knew it was a futile effort, but Thorvald wouldn't give up. Finally, near sunset, he bowed his head, and we turned toward shore.

We made landfall on a beach protected by soaring cliffs, and as we approached, we caught sight of an odd-looking rock sitting in the middle of a small bay to the north. The rock's white top reminded me of the squat white-headed seabirds abundant off the south shore of Greenland.

That night, we made camp on the rocky beach, just beyond the high-water mark. Archers were dispatched to the cliff tops to keep watch.

In the morning, we discovered a land covered with oak and several varieties of evergreens. Thankfully, the trees sat far enough apart, with little underbrush, to let us explore with ease. We soon came upon springs with the sweetest of water and a good-sized salt-free pond with water so cold that it numbed our fingers.

Shrubs, especially in the marshland surrounding the pond, were thick with early berries, making me sorry I wouldn't be there in late summer, when we could have harvested them for wine.

Seals sunned themselves on rocks offshore, the woods teemed

with rabbits, and there were birds everywhere. Gulls, as white as snow, swooped along the shoreline, cawing in the breeze, while more melodious birds sang from the trees. Brown-and-white ducks with shockingly orange beaks eyed us anxiously from the far edge of the pond. The strangest birds I had ever seen—full-bodied brown creatures with spindly legs, tiny heads, and slack red folds under their chins—strutted through the woods.

That magical place turned out to be an almost island. It was connected to the mainland by a long sandbar that was covered by the sea except at low tide.

The best news of all was that there was no sign of human habitation, as if no man before us had ever set foot in that paradise.

We kept camp on the beach again the second night, circling our leaned-in longships around our tents and the fire pit. We feasted on seal, rabbit, and that strange spindly legged bird, which tasted a good deal better than it looked. Then we slept deeply under a full moon while the archers kept watch from the cliff tops.

The following morning dawned bright and warm. First up, I made the discovery: Sveinn's body had washed up with the high tide and been deposited just below where Thorvald slept. The boy lay on his side with his knees pulled up slightly, as if taking a pleasant nap.

Thorvald saw this as a sign of divine favor. He knelt next to the body and prayed loudly to Odin, Thor, Michael the archangel, the Virgin Mary, and Jesus Christ. Like so many of us whose families had been converted to Christianity, we have never stopped venerating our old gods.

With tears in his eyes, Thorvald pointed to the giant rock formation that formed the southern boundary of the beach. The rock face was wildly irregular, with outcroppings and crevices, reminding me of a castle that had once appeared to me in a crazy dream.

"We'll bury him there," Thorvald announced to the hushed men.

Thorsten the carver was ordered to select a rune stone and begin work immediately. Meanwhile, the best climbers sought out a crevice on the castle rock suitable for the body.

We found the perfect stone sitting in the middle of the high meadow nearby, as if it were waiting for us. Unlike the dark rock formations making up the shoreline, this nearly translucent white boulder looked as if it had dropped out of the sky.

I believe it was Thorsten's best engraving ever. Long-bearded Thor, wielding his hammer in one hand and a lightning bolt in the other, was encircled by a serpent biting its tail. Red pigment made from Thorvald's own blood gave the image unimaginable beauty and power.

At dawn, we sealed the crevice with intricately interlocking stones and boarded our longships for the voyage north.

After shoving off, our rowers slowed to let the other vessels proceed while Thorvald, as imposing as a great ash tree with his red hair tousled by the breeze, stood astern for one last look back.

I caught him when he fell. A crimson-feathered arrow was stuck deep in his neck.

I was told later that the rowers drove us forward at unimagined speed while hundreds of natives whooped and drummed along the shoreline.

Even so, all I could take in was my master uttering his last words.

"I am a happy man favored by the gods. I will follow the boy into the next world." Then, making the sign of the cross, he fell silent.

We buried Thorvald on the southernmost of the Nine Sisters, two days away from that magical, terrible almost island. I was pleased that his body was not burned in the tradition of our pre-Christian days.

Then, with sadness never experienced before or since, we continued our voyage home.

# $\mathcal{T}$HE IGLOO

Pettigrew had been cutting ice for Mr. Tudor for several years, but this was his first trip to Squimset Lake. The Squimset was known to produce the best ice anywhere. It was so pure and flawless that it became Mr. Tudor's premier brand, gracing the most fashionable tables from Charleston to New Orleans and going for upward of twenty cents a pound.

Joining the Squimset ice-cutting gang looked like a promotion to Pettigrew, but neither the foreman nor even his brother, Liam, offered a word of congratulation to him about his new assignment.

It was a perfect day for harvesting ice: twenty-five degrees and solidly overcast. They were fortunate, since even a few minutes of filtered sunlight could melt ice on a subfreezing March day.

This was to be the first trial run of Mr. Tudor's ice plow. If it worked, it would mark the end of the backbreaking extraction of each chunk by hand. As Mr. Tudor had told the assembled men the day before, the plow was designed to produce ice blocks of uniform dimensions. Instead of loading irregular pieces into a ship's hold, they could fit the blocks closer together and reduce meltwater.

Tudor called meltwater a "devilish problem." Insulating each block with a generous coat of sawdust had already increased the amount of salable ice arriving in Havana the year before, the first time a shipment to Cuba had broken even. Speeding up the ice-cutting process and "spacing," as Tudor put it, could finally make exports of New England ice to the tropics a financial success.

A pair of parallel serrated blades were attached to the ends of the plow about two feet apart. One man led the horse in front while Liam, the designated cutter, guided the razor-sharp saws from behind. Pettigrew watched the horse being led slowly from one end of the lake to the other, with the plow leaving two perfectly carved lines in its wake. After about a dozen passes, the team moved to the edge of the pond ninety degrees away and began dividing the space into what looked like a giant chessboard. While the rest of the gang were busy prying the blocks out with crowbars, Liam proceeded to guide the ice plow over another section of the lake.

Looking up from his work, Pettigrew caught sight of Mr. Tudor alone on horseback, monitoring the proceedings from the shore. Though Tudor was not yet an old man, his unkempt hair was already as white as the snow on the ground around him. Combined with his perpetual scowl and pointed chin, the wild hair gave the man a fearsome and unpredictable aspect.

Pettigrew was helping to lift a block into a wagon, when a gunshot rang out from nearby woods.

"Damned hunters!" one of the gang grumbled.

The man leading the horse had the reins ripped from his hands as it panicked and bucked violently. From where he was, Pettigrew could see a piece of the plow fly off the ice and strike his brother.

"I'm a dead man!" Liam cried as they all ran toward him.

Pettigrew couldn't believe that a man could spill so much blood so fast and remain standing. The blade had caused a frightful injury, slicing into his brother's lower torso. Shredded clothing and a fist-sized piece of flesh lay at his feet as Liam clutched his privates, blood gushing between his fingers and staining the ice around him.

The men laid Liam on the ice, all the while reassuring him that it was only a minor wound, and he'd be fine. Meanwhile, Pettigrew frantically poked fingers, hands, handkerchiefs, gloves, and even a pocket watch into the wound to staunch the flow, but the blood seeped through everything. He was amazed by its warmth and saltiness as it sprayed his face. When it was over, the other men stood back reverently while Pettigrew lay atop the still body and wept.

As soon as they helped him to his feet, he scanned the shoreline for Mr. Tudor.

"Galloped away," one of the men snarled.

Liam's funeral was held at Saint Patrick's Church in the middle of Squimset's Irishtown. Pettigrew sat in the front pew with Liam's widow and her two daughters while Father Cassidy, clearly on the verge of tears himself, celebrated the Mass.

Father Cassidy began his sermon with a sober recitation of what had happened to Liam before reminding everyone of how devoted the man had been to Dora and his daughters; how he'd sing his way through a day's labor; how he'd laugh at a good joke until tears came to his eyes; and how God's plans for every one of us were beyond all understanding. He pledged that the parish community would keep Liam in their hearts forever and do everything possible physically and spiritually for the family he left behind.

Then his tone changed. In an instant, reverence and reminiscence gave way to heated words with flashes of fury.

"We are the forgotten ones!" he thundered. "They hand us the punishing and dangerous work they don't care to do themselves and then treat us like dogs."

If a man "on the other side of the tracks" had been in such an accident, he went on, the newspapers would have carried the story, and the mayor would have come to share in their grief. Irishtown, however, would be expected to endure this tragedy alone.

Earlier that morning, a messenger had delivered an envelope for

Dora containing a draft for sixty dollars from a Boston bank, signed by Frederic Tudor. There was no accompanying note.

Pettigrew had already become an integral part of his brother's family by then. Since the day he'd sailed into Boston a few years earlier, he'd shared meals, played with the children, and slept on a pallet in Liam's kitchen, so there were few practical adjustments to make.

No one was surprised when Bartholomew Pettigrew married Liam's widow, Dora, barely four months after the ice-cutting accident. An unmarried sibling was expected to do just that, but everyone knew that this exceptional couple agreed to wed more out of affection than obligation.

Well-wishers packed Saint Patrick's for the ceremony on a sweltering July afternoon.

It was the first time in years that Pettigrew would use his given name, which he detested, and it would be years more before he'd be required to use it again.

Until the time of the accident, Pettigrew had found work with Tudor only during ice-cutting season. The remainder of the year, he'd picked up jobs wherever he could find them, clearing land for new roads and railroad lines or shoveling snow for the town of Squimset after winter storms.

However, soon after the wedding, he was hired as a gardener for Mr. Tudor's cottage in Egg Rock. A village in the town of Squimset, Egg Rock, which consisted of two islands connected to mainland by a sandbar, was named after an oddly shaped rock that jutted out of the ocean nearby. He was hired for a seasonal position that would end at first frost in October.

But when fall arrived, the foreman gave Pettigrew the news that he'd be needed year-round. He added that on Tudor's orders, Pettigrew would never cut ice again.

Soon after coming to Egg Rock, Pettigrew learned about Frederic Tudor's marriage to Euphemia Fenno. An item about the wedding—"a small family affair at the bride's home in New York"—appeared in the Boston newspapers.

When the Tudors arrived in Egg Rock the following spring, the gardening crew couldn't stop wagging their tongues about it.

Frederic was fifty, and Euphemia was barely nineteen!

She was a handsome, full-figured woman with jet-black hair, startling green eyes, and an open, warm countenance. Pettigrew saw little of Mrs. Tudor. She stayed out of sight while her husband, restless as always, shuttled back and forth from Boston by boat, on horseback, and, on occasion, on foot. The tongue waggers opined that Mr. Tudor was enjoying other female companionship back in the city and speculated that Mrs. Tudor had married in the hopes of a long and affluent widowhood.

Tudor had visited Egg Rock as a boy and apparently been smitten with what amounted to a square mile of windblown pasture sitting in the middle of the ocean. His father had called Egg Rock a godforsaken place, but the boy announced his intention to build his "manse" there someday.

In this, he was good to his word. Tudor's manse was already up and running the year Pettigrew started as gardener. Everyone called the place the Igloo but never in Mr. Tudor's presence. The name captured the essence of the place since the rough-hewn granite blocks of its facade gave it an ungainly and unfinished look, and its occupant, the Ice King, seemed as foreign and unapproachable as an Eskimo.

Mr. Tudor's new home in Egg Rock did not go unnoticed by his fellow Bostonians.

As the city grew and open space disappeared, Boston's summers became unbearable. The heat alone was torture enough, but the Charles River, little more than an open sewer, gave off a horrid stench night and day. Once steamboats were introduced, Egg Rock, no more than an hour's passage from downtown, provided the perfect escape for those who could afford it. Moneyed Beacon Hill and Back Bay families either stayed at the new hotel on East Point or bought up land nearby.

Businessmen, lawyers, and bankers started building summer cottages on the eastern end of the big island. The poet Longfellow and John Fremont, hero of the Mexican War, were said to be interested. A Protestant church was being planned, and a long wooden staircase was built so the new residents could access the neighborhood's spectacular beach nestled between soaring cliffs.

Tudor's business, which had introduced ice to places where people could only dream of frozen water, had just completed its most profitable season. He was expanding his markets to London and, from what Pettigrew had heard, had plans to export his ice halfway around the world to Calcutta.

If Pettigrew expected Tudor to be too occupied with his business ventures to find time for Egg Rock, he was mistaken. After telling him about his year-round employment, the foreman led Pettigrew to the Igloo's veranda, where Mr. Tudor was waiting.

Mr. Tudor scrutinized Pettigrew from head to toe before breaking the silence. "You look able enough, and you were blessed with not too Irish a name. And I have been told that you don't speak with too thick a brogue."

The younger man wondered how much more Tudor knew about him.

Tudor pointed to a pathetically scrawny sapling close to the house, out of the wind. "I am given to understand that you know more about trees than anyone else around. How can I get my apple trees to grow out here?"

"Pair each young tree, sir, with a fast-grower. The fast-grower protects a sapling like a big brother. I've seen plenty of balm of Gileads hereabouts. Farmers call them trash trees and are happy to be rid of them. One of them should do a fine job protecting this russet."

Pettigrew explained that he'd learned about such pairings in Ireland, another windy place. He began to explain the technique in detail, but Tudor raised his hand in protest.

"Enough!" Tudor smiled for an instant, reminding Pettigrew of a momentary parting of clouds on a blustery day.

But the interview wasn't over. He settled into a chair, gestured for Pettigrew to sit, and began to speak.

"In colonial times, Egg Rock provided Squimset with firewood and lumber. Once the trees were gone, it became the town's common pasture."

He paused and closed his eyes. "Since I was a child, I've had a recurring dream in which I am the first explorer to drop anchor at Egg Rock. I'm dazzled by a headland covered with a small forest, brilliant green in the spring sunshine."

He intended to restore Egg Rock to its natural state by reforesting it with thousands of trees, and he expected Pettigrew to carry out his orders.

Sensing that the interview was finally over, Pettigrew stood. However, Tudor had one last question. "What's your favorite variety?"

"The copper beech, sir, the grandest of trees."

Tudor pointed to the Igloo's front entrance. "Plant the very best you can find right there."

Pettigrew turned out to be a solid choice for the full-time gardener's job since he could attach a name to any growing thing and make just about anything he stuck in the ground sprout and grow. His skills quickly gained the respect of the other men, but it was his gentle disposition that won them over.

He advanced quickly. He was promoted to assistant foreman of the grounds crew in the spring—but for only a few weeks. One day the foreman got into an argument with Mr. Tudor, who fired him on the spot. Pettigrew took his place.

The foreman was expected to be available day and night, which was an impossibility for someone living on the other side of the sandbar leading to the mainland. As soon as his predecessor departed, the Pettigrew family, including their newborn son, Liam, moved into the redbrick foreman's cottage. It sat a few minutes' walk down the hill from the Igloo, close to Bear Pond, the island's only pool of fresh water.

Neither Pettigrew nor Dora had ever lived in a real house before.

Tudor had a reputation for going through employees at an alarming rate. With that in mind, Dora was wary of leaving Irishtown. Although she dreamed of escaping their rat-infested tenement, it would come to nothing if Pettigrew got sacked like all the others.

"Don't worry, Dora. If I can convince him that my ideas are actually his, he'll be satisfied."

Pettigrew's strategy seemed to work, since he remained foreman at the Igloo and Mr. Tudor's assistant for nearly thirty years.

Remarkably, in the course of hundreds of conversations that took place between the two men, Tudor never said one word about the accident at Squimset Lake and never once uttered Liam's name.

The reforestation of Egg Rock proceeded by fits and starts. The pasture land turned out to be more hostile to young trees than Pettigrew had expected. Salt air didn't poison trees, as some naysayers claimed, but the constant wind nearly did. Pettigrew and his men constructed a glass-roofed greenhouse for the youngest plants before transplanting them to fenced-in gardens for another season until he could finally plant each tree with its balm of Gilead protector.

The system worked.

By the end of the fifth planting season, Pettigrew had more than four thousand healthy young trees—elms, maples, willows, sassafras, oaks, hickory, poplar, and beech—in stock, as well as nearly two hundred protector trees. If he were to plant them in a row, he explained to Dora, the row would stretch over the sandbar from the Igloo to Saint Patrick's Church in Squimset and back again.

Tudor sped up the reforestation process by offering trees to homeowners for free if they planted them on their property. Even the bluebloods of East Point, who considered the Ice King an unpredictable, testy eccentric, came around. After all, they were men of the world who recognized a good deal when it appeared under their noses.

Egg Rock Road, the island's only thoroughfare, stretched from the end of the sandbar eastward to Forty Steps, which was named after the beach's wooden staircase. Tudor set out to transform it to a Grande Allée with parallel rows of stately American elms.

By the time little Liam was old enough to join his father on his daily rounds, Egg Rock already looked more like a park than a cow pasture.

Tudor was a restless man with a bottomless reservoir of energy. He was apt to appear at the Igloo without warning, having walked the eighteen miles from his home in Boston.

He always brought along a new idea or two for Pettigrew to work on. He ordered tobacco plants from the Carolinas, but his hoped-for cash crop was meager, and the chewing tobacco they produced was too pungent for even the toughest man. Undeterred, he ordered a shipment of cotton plants, convinced that the expanding New England textile industry would snatch up locally grown cotton. However, the crop failed, Pettigrew's green thumb notwithstanding.

Meanwhile, Pettigrew came up with a novel idea of his own. Egg Rock's most prominent landmark was the rock itself, sitting offshore. Soon after moving out there, he'd asked a couple of townspeople why the rock was so named, since it was shaped less like an egg than a half-submerged potato.

"The birds lay their eggs there," one had said.

"No, it's the color!" a second had insisted. "All those bird droppings have turned the damned thing into an enormous outhouse."

Pettigrew told Tudor about that conversation and the ready supply of fertilizer a half mile away. The old man nodded gravely and walked away without a word.

Days later, the first barrel of Egg Rock guano was delivered to the foreman's workshop.

Later, Tudor credited their success to four innovations: the greenhouse, the wind fences, the balm of Gilead protectors, and Egg Rock's guano, which, mixed with compost so as not to burn the roots, they liberally sprinkled into each hole before a new tree was planted.

Pettigrew had been purchasing plants, trees, and all manner of gardening supplies for years and keeping a running account of expenditures in a ledger that Tudor reviewed at the beginning of each month. At those sessions in Tudor's study behind the parlor on the Igloo's ground floor, the old man would adjust his spectacles and scrutinize the entries, running his finger down each page, while Pettigrew stood. Once satisfied, he'd write out a draft for the outstanding amount and dismiss his assistant with a nod.

One day he pointed to a pile of books and papers on his desk. "Now that I've nearly filled Egg Rock with trees, Pettigrew, I have another job for you. I don't know how a mere gardener knows so much about bookkeeping, but you do—and that's all that matters. From now on, you'll be keeping the books on everything here in Egg Rock."

Pettigrew and Liam had been brought up on a large English manor in Kilkenny, where their father, once the head gardener, had been the resident superintendent.

Mr. Pettigrew had been in charge of the manor's purchases, which he carefully entered into a huge leather-bound ledger. Once a month—except when Bartholomew, the duke of Gilesworth, was back in London—he'd transport the ledger, wrapped in linen to keep it clean and dry, in a wheelbarrow up to the manor house for the duke's perusal.

Liam had shown little aptitude for numbers, but when Mr. Pettigrew had seen that his younger son was interested, he'd taught the boy how to enter expenditures line by line in the debit column, tally them up, and enter the reimbursements in the credit column to balance the books.

Pettigrew's education hadn't stopped there. His father, who could name the genus and species of any tree he saw and coax the most stubborn plant to take root and prosper, taught the boy everything he knew.

Later, while sawing ice on a New England pond, Pettigrew tried to forget how much else he had learned.

Until Liam's accident changed everything.

Father Aloysius Cassidy had been recruited from Maryland, where the first American Catholic seminary was up and running. He arrived at Saint Patrick's only weeks before Liam was killed.

Saint Patrick's was the only Catholic parish between Boston and Salem and sat in the middle of Squimset's Irishtown, one of the most desperate immigrant communities in the country. To make matters worse, back home blight was wiping out the potato crop, the mainstay of the Irish diet, leading to mass starvation. Desperate Irish refugees escaping the Great Hunger began pouring into slums stretching from Baltimore to Boston.

Newly ordained, Father Cassidy made up for his inexperience with an uncanny talent for showing up just where he was most needed. He seemed to be everywhere at once, day and night, making some of the faithful wonder if he, like the mystical saints, had been blessed with the gift of bilocation.

Cassidy's flock was a tough bunch. One in five perished on the ships, but the odds of surviving the New World ghettos were little better. The end could come slowly with consumption or drink or without warning when typhoid or diphtheria swept through the tenements, or a robber on the street outside the door could take one's life in an instant. The hardest losses for Father Cassidy were mothers dying in childbirth, just as his own mother had the day he was born.

Still, Liam Pettigrew's gruesome death plunged that battle-hardened neighborhood into unprecedented mourning—and provided Father Cassidy with his first test.

He rushed to the ice-covered lake as soon as he heard the news, accompanied Liam's body home, and stayed with the family throughout the ordeals of the wake and funeral.

Although Pettigrew and Dora had moved across the sandbar to Egg Rock, they never left Irishtown behind.

On Sundays, they piled into one of the Igloo's horse-drawn carts for the trip to Saint Patrick's, and on Thursdays, when he could get away, the priest rode out for family supper at the foreman's cottage.

Over those suppers, the two men, brought up thousands of miles apart, discovered how much they had in common.

Aloysius Cassidy, the son of Irish immigrants, had been brought up in Baltimore's version of Irishtown. His father ran a small grocery store down one flight from where they lived. Before he could do much of anything else, little Lou swept the floor under the watchful eyes of his four older sisters.

Along with the parish church next door and the tavern across the way, Cassidy's Corner was a neighborhood institution.

His father, rumpled and bespectacled, presided over his cash box and account book at the counter while his sisters stocked shelves and waited on customers.

The space was filled from floor to ceiling with meats and produce; brooms and mops; tableware and candles; and, in a small annex in the back, shirts, trousers, frocks, and shoes. The place was jammed with old and young but too few paying customers. Mr. Cassidy had such a big heart and so many people on credit penciled into his account book that the store barely kept afloat.

He was so inclined to let people charge things that no one took the trouble to steal.

Young Aloysius, expected to run the business someday, learned arithmetic from his father's account books. He could navigate a double-entry ledger or inventory a dozen shelves of dry goods before he could write a declarative sentence.

He also learned that Mr. Cassidy, forever scribbling names and numbers in his account book, was as looked up to as the parish priest and the neighborhood midwife.

With his endless acts of kindness, Mr. Cassidy was unwittingly preparing his son for the priesthood.

The day he arrived in Irishtown, Father Cassidy unpacked his brand-new account book, a gift from his father. He'd heard stories about his predecessor's disdain for money—"The Lord will always provide," he'd said—but he would damn well know where every one of Saint Patrick's pennies ended up.

In Irishtown, where there had been no bankers, insurance agents, or social workers, Father Aloysius Cassidy became all three overnight.

The Tudor family grew quickly. As one of Pettigrew's men put it, it was as if Mr. Tudor were making up for lost time.

Dora and her two daughters, Margaret and Genevieve, helped care for the Tudor children, which allowed Pettigrew to get acquainted with the little Tudors. In time, they seemed to spend more time at the foreman's cottage than at the Igloo.

From what Pettigrew heard, Euphemia would spend days alone in her room, reading. One of the tongue waggers added, "She's better at making babies than carin' for 'em."

Summer after summer, cholera swept through cities to the south but spared Boston. That led eminent preachers of the city to declare the Athens of America was a special place under God's protection. Then, in Pettigrew's tenth year in Egg Rock, the sickness swooped down on Irishtown. Father Cassidy and a trio of Sisters of Charity from the nearby convent went from home to home, ministering to the sick and aiding the bereaved, but in reality, there was little they could do. Whole families, healthy in the morning, could be dead by nightfall. Thankfully, the outbreak left as abruptly as it had arrived—but only after carrying off more than three hundred souls.

Two of the sisters perished, but the priest and the last nun, Sister Benedicta, miraculously survived.

It took weeks for Father Cassidy to get strong enough to ride out to Egg Rock.

Never robust, he was left with barely any flesh clinging to his bones. Dora gasped when she laid eyes on him.

The priest asked Pettigrew to accompany him to Bear Pond while Dora put the children to bed.

Pettigrew, like everyone in Egg Rock, knew that Irishtown had been put under quarantine as soon as the cholera struck, with streets leading into the neighborhood barricaded and guarded by the constabulary. That evening, the priest told him the rest of the story. The authorities had orders to shoot on sight anyone crossing the barricades, and they'd killed a confused old man wandering through a checkpoint.

No one was allowed to cross into Irishtown. "No doctors, no nurses, no lawmen, and nobody to help us bury our dead." The priest pulled on his friend's sleeve for emphasis. "They wanted every one of us to die!"

Pettigrew hadn't seen Cassidy so fired up since he'd given Liam's funeral sermon years earlier.

A dozen mallards paddled lazily to the other side of the pond as the men approached.

At the pond's edge, the priest lowered his voice, as if the ducks might overhear. "I have a plan."

It took Cassidy a few minutes to explain, and once he finished, Pettigrew nodded in agreement.

Later that night, Pettigrew told Dora.

She nodded her assent, but slowly. "I feel we'll regret this" was all she would say.

Pettigrew and his family resumed their trips to Saint Patrick's for Sunday Mass, with one small change in the routine: once a month, Pettigrew slipped the priest an envelope filled with cash.

Cholera never returned to Irishtown, making Pettigrew wonder if his friend's prayers were finally being answered. The city's plan to pipe fresh water into its neighborhoods also made a difference. The water department didn't include Irishtown at first, which necessitated a visit to city hall by Father Cassidy—carrying a bulging billfold—to straighten things out.

So, other than accepting a bribe to supply fresh water, Squimset let Irishtown fend for itself.

With Saint Patrick's financially stable for the first time, Pettigrew watched Cassidy set up a grammar school, with his fellow cholera survivor, Sister Benedicta, as principal. Church attendance mushroomed with more immigrants escaping the continuing famine back home. Among the newcomers Cassidy found carpenters, stone masons, and roofers to enlarge the church; former soldiers to form a neighborhood watch; teachers for the new school; and laborers to clean the streets.

If the priest had a payroll for all this charitable work, he kept no record of it.

The bishop came up from Boston and was greeted by an overflow crowd, including dozens on whom he conferred the sacrament of confirmation. That must have made an impression, since a freshly ordained priest soon arrived as Saint Patrick's first curate, or assistant priest, to help out.

Around that time, Father Cassidy invited Pettigrew to another after-supper walk to Bear Pond. It was already dark, but the nearly full moon transformed the pond into a big silver disk that reminded Pettigrew of a giant, highly polished silver dollar.

After that, the monthly envelopes stopped being delivered to Irishtown—and Pettigrew was finally able to sleep through the night.

The next step was to dispose of the second ledger, which Pettigrew had hidden in the stone barn next to the foreman's cottage. It took days for him to find the right time to bury it deep under his vegetable garden, but when he climbed up to the hayloft, it was missing.

His brother, Liam, had called him even-keeled since the day Pettigrew calmly led the horses out of a burning barn back in Ireland. He'd remained composed when the immigrant ship nearly broke apart during a violent storm and even on that frightful morning when Liam lay bleeding to death on the ice at Squimset Lake.

When he discovered that the second ledger was missing, he experienced heart-pounding panic for the first time in his life. He waited for something to happen, for the other shoe to drop, as Dora said, but nothing did. Eventually, he adjusted to the prospect of never knowing who had taken the ledger—or why.

With his business empire expanding, Mr. Tudor spent fewer days in Egg Rock, and weeks went by without Pettigrew getting even a glimpse of him. Every month or so, Pettigrew would be summoned to Mr. Tudor's study for a review of the accounts. At each meeting, Pettigrew wondered if the other shoe would finally drop, but it never did.

Egg Rock seceded from the town of Squimset during Pettigrew's thirtieth year of working in Egg Rock. Many in Egg Rock felt that the Squimset authorities failed to provide them with adequate services. Even Tudor, who rarely spoke publicly about anything, called Egg Rock "Squimset's stepchild." Pettigrew was reminded of Father Cassidy, who had proclaimed that the people of Irishtown were "the forgotten ones."

The town celebrated its independence with a Fourth of July parade, during which the town's newly elected selectmen planned to honor Mr. Tudor as Egg Rock's greatest benefactor.

Tudor had not been well, and it was unclear whether he'd be able to make the trip from Boston for the event, so when a carriage carrying Mr. and Mrs. Tudor led the procession along Egg Rock Road, the cheering was spontaneous and heartfelt.

After the ceremony, at town hall, Tudor spotted Pettigrew in the crowd and motioned him over.

"Come see me in Boston," he whispered, "tomorrow."

The Tudor town house sat a block from the statehouse at the top of Beacon Hill, a short walk from the train depot. The ornate, bow-windowed three-story edifice had little in common with the rough-hewn granite cottage in Egg Rock. *The house of a dandy*, Pettigrew thought as a maid ushered him into Tudor's study. The blinds were drawn, and it took him a moment to make out Mr. Tudor in the semidarkness. He was seated in a high-backed chair and pointed to an empty chair nearby. "Move that chair closer so you can hear me." His gravelly voice was no louder than a whisper.

The maid drew back the curtains, letting late morning sunlight flood the room.

The missing account book sat on a small table next to him, and when Tudor caught his foreman staring at it, he smiled for only the second time in Pettigrew's experience. "Don't worry, Pettigrew. I knew all along."

Tea was served, and once they were alone, Tudor explained that his youngest daughter, Viola, had found "a book" while playing hide-and-seek in the hayloft of the foreman's barn and carried it back to the Igloo.

"The child had no idea what it was," he continued, "other than it was pretty. And in a way, it was."

*The other shoe*, Pettigrew thought, wondering if the police were in the next room, about to barge in and arrest him.

"Euphemia brought it to me right away and, I must say, just in time. I had already discovered discrepancies in the accounts and was about to send you packing. I don't know if she looked at it first, and I don't plan to ask."

The old man lifted his cup and looked at Pettigrew as if he were offering a toast. "You entered twelve monthly payments to Saint Patrick's Church. Why did you stop?"

"They're self-sufficient now, sir. In time, they can pay you back."

Tudor shook his head with obvious irritation and pointed to the table. "Open the book, Pettigrew."

Tucked inside was a deed to the foreman's cottage, signed over to Bartholomew Pettigrew.

On the return train, Pettigrew clutched the newfound account book like a parent of a wayward child, and time and again, he felt for the deed safely hidden in his pocket.

Back at Egg Rock, he stood gazing at the redbrick cottage, trying to absorb the news before sharing it with Dora.

At supper, she brought out the Christmas wine, and Pettigrew raised his glass.

"God bless Frederic Tudor!"

"Amen," replied Dora with tears in her eyes.

Once it grew dark, they buried the book deep under their vegetable garden.

A month later, Tudor was dead. Pettigrew learned about it from the newspaper, just as he'd learned about Tudor's marriage to Euphemia Fenno decades earlier. He'd died of pneumonia, the obituary stated, and a committal service and burial would be held at King's Chapel.

Pettigrew was preparing seedlings in the hothouse on a March afternoon—*A fine ice-cutting day*, he thought, studying the overcast sky through the glass roof—when officers arrived with a search warrant for "the foreman's cottage on the property of the late Mr. Frederic Tudor, at present occupied by Bartholomew Pettigrew."

The constable, a man Pettigrew had known since his first days in Egg Rock, gave him an apologetic smile.

When he learned that they had gone to Saint Patrick's rectory earlier that day, Pettigrew was grateful that Father Cassidy was not alive to witness the scene.

They took papers from the foreman's cottage and other objects from Pettigrew's desk.

Lagging behind the others as he departed, the constable drew Pettigrew aside and told him that a complaint of embezzlement had been lodged at the superior court in Boston by one Euphemia Fenno.

"That's what she calls herself these days. Do you know what the rest of the world calls her?"

"No."

"The Ice Queen."

He tipped his hat to his old friend before running to catch up with the others.

# 𝒯HE CASTLE

Ezra Newhall joined the others on the Castle's veranda to watch the parade's approach.

"They're calling this their Wide Awake Rally," the widow announced to the hotel guests, as if it hadn't been the talk of Egg Rock for days.

She turned to Ezra and lowered her voice. "I'm glad Johnny isn't here yet. He never cared for parades, with their trumped-up frivolity. He may be a redhead like his father, but he's always been serious in a way his father never was."

John Ellsworth, one of the country's most famous men, was expected the next day. The widow had already vacated her room off the lobby and would occupy guest quarters upstairs during his stay.

He hadn't visited Egg Rock in years, and she'd told Ezra she wanted to make his homecoming a special time.

Ezra pointed out a dozen points of light approaching from the east side of the island. "They'll be here soon."

When the marchers filed onto Black Rock Wharf at the foot of the hill, the band launched into the stirring "Lincoln and Freedom." Torches swayed in time with the drumbeat while trumpets, sounding crisp and martial in the night air, sounded as seductive a call to arms as Ezra had ever heard.

He pictured himself, hardly more than a boy, standing guard over supply wagons in Georgetown on another August night much like this. As he watched Washington burn in the distance, a carriage carrying Mrs. Madison emerged from the smoke on its way to safety across the Potomac. The men stood at attention as she flew by.

Later, he'd hear that the president's wife had ordered that the paintings from the president's house be cut from their frames so she could carry them on her lap as she sped out of the city.

The hotel guests whooped and hollered their support for Mr. Lincoln's torchbearers while Ezra stood quietly, trying to shake the image of Washington in flames.

Ezra Newhall had never learned a formal trade but was known as a first-class odd-jobber. He could calm a horse, ride a mule, milk a cow, gut a mackerel, pull a lobster pot, mend a sleeve, cobble a shoe, paint a barn, build a wall, calk the seams and ribs of any boat, glaze a window, read a sextant, patch a roof, bind a wound, lance a boil, trim a sail, and perform a thousand other little tasks.

If anyplace cried out for such a jack-of-all trades, it was Egg Rock's sprawling, jerry-built Castle.

He'd spent his childhood at his father's shoemaking shop, a weather-beaten shack high on Curlew Beach at the east end of town. On his sixteenth birthday, his father informed him that he was an octoroon, a word he'd never heard before. That meant, his father explained, that exactly one-eighth of Ezra's blood was Negro.

"Simple arithmetic," Hiram Newhall explained. Ezra's great-grandmother was a Negress; his grandmother was a mulatto; and his mother, whom Ezra never knew, was a quadroon.

The old man, with a malignant tumor devouring his face and jaw, propped himself up on pillows. "You need to know this, Ezzy."

He grunted out each word with heroic effort. "So you don't get a nasty surprise the day your child is born."

As far as Ezra could tell, this strange news had no effect on the way he conducted his life. In the beginning, he'd study his face in the mirror, checking whether his nose was too wide, his lips were too thick, or his hair was too tightly curled. He knew he looked like everybody else, but he could never quite banish the thought of being kidnapped, carried south in chains, and sold at auction. He dreamed about finding a doctor who could magically bleed him of the tainted one-eighth and make him whole again.

When his father died, the little shoemaking shop died with him. Squimset, the city on the other end of the sandbar linking Egg Rock to the mainland, was already becoming a shoemaking center. Its larger shops, with three or four workers, were more efficient than Hiram Newhall's solo operation could ever be.

As luck would have it, the army was recruiting men for the new war against England, so the day after he buried his father, Private Ezra Newhall was mustered into an artillery battalion and sent to a garrison outside Washington.

When the war was over, he came home and married Abby May, an Egg Rock girl he'd known as long as he could remember. After Abby and their baby boy died in childbirth, the widow took him in.

Ezra slept in a tiny room at the top of the house, which he entered by climbing a ladder at the end of the hallway on the third story. The room had barely enough space for a bed, washstand, and trunk, but a large window filled its west-facing wall, giving him a fine view of Squimset Harbor and the Seal Rocks. The rocks were visible for only a few hours each day, at low tide. As soon as they broke through the water's surface, dozens of seals would appear, sunning themselves or slipping in and out of the water.

Summer and winter, in sunlight or a gale-driven rain, the Seal Rocks held to their own rhythm. He didn't need to consult tide tables to know when he could drive over the sandbar to Squimset. When the rocks were visible, the road was open. He got in the habit of carrying an old spyglass in his pocket—to check the tides, he told the widow. The truth, he knew, was more complicated. Keeping watch over the rocks steadied him.

Ezra ferried guests to and from Black Rock Wharf and Squimset, for a stroll around Mr. Tudor's orchards, or for a climb down Forty

Steps, a wooden staircase leading to Ezra's favorite beach. On the finest summer days, he'd find time to lead them down the path to the shore below the Castle for picnics and tide pooling.

The tide pools, indentations in the rock where water remained at low tide, were lined with barnacles, periwinkles, and bright green seaweed. The visitors delighted in overturning rocks to find little crabs skittering away. After rowing a few yards offshore, Ezra showed them how to thread a bit of clam on a hook and wait for a tug on the line.

By then, Egg Rock had become a well-known summer resort, attracting visitors not only from Boston but from as far away as New York and Philadelphia. It was no longer the backwater it once had been. The widow was fond of telling the story about an early citizen of Egg Rock who, when he heard news of the Battle of Lexington, jumped on his horse to join the Minutemen. Alas, he arrived after everyone had gone home.

Now, with the imminent return of the renowned John Ellsworth, Egg Rock was in little danger of becoming a backwater ever again.

The Castle was buzzing. With the presidential campaign under way, much of the talk centered on Lincoln, an ungainly backwoods politician from Illinois. From his perch on his trolley or while attending to guests in the dining room, Ezra listened. The widow insisted on civil discourse at the Castle, but she had no control beyond its walls.

On one trip to Squimset, he pulled off the road to physically separate two guests who had expressed opposite opinions regarding the South's right to secede.

Widow Ellsworth might not have been a widow at all. Instead of clarifying matters by drawing his last breath in his own bed, John Ellsworth Senior had run off to make his fortune in the newly formed Republic of Texas, leaving nothing behind but a pile of gambling debts. Soon she was taking in boarders to support herself and her young son. Once word got around that the widow's rooming house was clean and respectable, she devised ways to accommodate more guests.

Before long, the old house doubled in size, with a haphazard jumble of rooms, corridors, and staircases. An early visitor jokingly called it the Castle, and the name stuck.

The gargantuan hotels on the east end of Egg Rock—the grand

hotels, as the widow put it—boasted hundreds of rooms. Those genuine castles featured restaurants for every taste, bars, floor shows, cotillions, concerts, lectures, magic shows, barbershops, and bowling alleys, and unlike her clientele of schoolteachers, bookkeepers, and traveling salesmen, the swells out on East Point were as grand as their surroundings.

As modest as the Castle was—it was the widow's home after all—she had her standards. Although a large bowl of rum punch appeared in the parlor right after supper—excluding Sundays—and was refilled liberally as the evening progressed, drunkenness, rowdiness, foul language, or ungentlemanly behavior toward the opposite sex resulted in the offender's abrupt departure on Ezra's trolley at the break of dawn.

The widow's front office was the big kitchen at the back of the house. From there, in the midst of preparing breakfast and dinner, she kept tabs on the chambermaids, dish washers, and serving girls. Peddlers came by with produce from the small farms and orchards near Bear Pond; clams, mussels, and crabs from the island's beaches; and lobsters pulled from pots just offshore. In the midst of such chaos, she always found time to greet new guests on arrival and wave a sad goodbye at their departure.

Ezra and the widow worked so well together that any visitor would have taken them for a long-wedded couple, were it not for the black silk dress the widow wore every day.

Black Rock Wharf, site of the torchlight parade the night before, sat on a rocky outcropping at the foot of the Castle's hilltop. It was the favored docking point for the Boston steamers because it jutted into twenty-five to thirty feet of Squimset Harbor, depending on the tides. It was also home for Egg Rock's best fishermen, who provided the Castle with the choicest cod, halibut, and stripers.

The air had turned oddly sultry for late summer, and the sky, vivid blue earlier, had turned milk white. Ezra noticed that the gulls, usually cawing and cavorting in huge loops over arriving fishing boats, had disappeared.

Waiting for the paddle-wheeler from Boston to appear at the

mouth of Squimset Harbor, Ezra thought back to the summer he'd spent with John Ellsworth. Ezra had just started work for the widow when Johnny arrived to spend the summer in Egg Rock. Through a friend of his Texas-bound father, he had started as an apprentice at a law office in Boston, and he would be returning to the city in the fall. The Castle was no more than a rooming house in those days, but the teenage boy, self-conscious and bookish, avoided the few guests as much as possible.

Just as his own father had, Ezra taught the boy how to scout out the best fishing spots, identify a clam's keyhole in wet sand, and catch the biggest crabs at low tide. However, Johnny spent most of that summer in the kitchen, baking bread or stirring the chowder pot. The widow joked he'd make a better chef than a lawyer.

One afternoon, Ezra returned from Squimset to find the widow pacing the veranda.

"He's on the steamer to Boston," she announced with a shake of her head. Before Ezra could ask why, she hurried back to the kitchen. The boy had planned to stay another week.

Ezra was dumbfounded. For the first time since he'd lost Abby May and the baby, he'd felt part of a family. He also knew the widow and the boy had felt the same.

The widow never spoke about Johnny's departure and rarely uttered her son's name after that.

For his part, Ezra knew enough not to ask.

John Ellsworth might have been away for twenty years, but he was no Rip Van Winkle. The shy teenager had become a successful lawyer, an eloquent antislavery orator, and a leader of the abolitionist cause.

Like a proud father, Ezra read everything he could about him in the newspapers and in pamphlets brought by guests to the Castle. Whenever Johnny's name came up in dinner conversations, Ezra hung on every word. He was proud of how the boy he'd once known had made his name by defending fugitive slaves and railing against the evils of slavery, often to indifferent or hostile audiences.

What pleased Ezra most, however, was John Ellsworth's passionate opposition to war.

Seeing Washington burn once was enough for him.

The day Johnny's letter arrived from Boston, Ezra overheard the widow singing when he passed by the kitchen: "Home again, Home again, from a foreign shore, And oh! It fills my heart with joy!" He had forgotten how beautiful her voice was.

When the middle-aged gentleman stepped off the Boston steamer, there was no question who he was. His red hair had barely dulled, although his generous mutton-chop whiskers had begun to gray. However, Ezra was astounded he'd forgotten the one thing that set John Ellsworth apart from most everyone else: he was cross-eyed.

The defect, which caused his right eye to turn slightly inward, was barely noticeable as a rule. Only when he became anxious or, as the widow once observed, he was hiding something would the eye go off-kilter.

He was dressed in a heavy dark suit, looking like an itinerant preacher who had voyaged from the North Pole. He had publicly renounced wearing cotton or consuming cane sugar, Ezra recalled, since both were produced by slave labor. His clothes hung loosely, as if he'd lost weight.

"Hello! I'm John Ellsworth!" he exclaimed in an orator's baritone that belonged to a man twice his bulk. He appeared to be looking over Ezra's left shoulder as he spoke, giving no indication that he remembered his old friend.

With the steamer trunk strapped safely on board, they made their way up the winding gravel drive to the Castle. Ezra had rehearsed a few words of welcome, but they would need to wait.

The widow was standing on the veranda, waiting. She smiled as her son alighted from the trolley, but her hands were clasped tightly together, white and bloodless.

Each evening, the guests assembled outside the dining room in their finest attire. Dinner remained the widow's secret until the serving girls carried the oversize china platters, tureens, and chafing dishes to the dining room buffet and went to work.

To celebrate John's return, the widow had prepared his favorite dishes: quahog chowder, fried oysters, roast duck, lobster pie, and peach cobbler.

He sat at the head of the table, wearing the same clothes he'd worn on the boat. Ezra had wondered if dinner talk would be stifled by the presence of such a luminary, but he needn't have worried. John Ellsworth had mastered the art of social intercourse.

Talk turned to the torchlit Wide Awake Rally of the previous evening.

*Thrilling, heroic,* and *patriotic* were some of the words echoing across the table. "Union now, Union forever!" exclaimed a boy who, Ezra believed, had been coached by his mother. They waited for the guest of honor to respond.

Finally, he rose. "I'll speak plainly. Union with the slave states is doomed. Why prolong the experiment? The South has the right to secede. I welcome secession because only then will our country be rid of the evil of slavery."

With that, the conversations went on, more heated than ever. When the wind picked up, rattling the window panes, no one at the table seemed to notice. Ezra and one of the serving girls hurried out to the veranda to rescue the rockers and wicker tables being tossed around. Sheets of rain pounded the house, and it grew so dark that they lit the candles an hour earlier than usual.

The parlor door flew open, and a servant quickly secured it by wedging a high-backed chair under the faulty knob. In the pause that followed, John stood again.

"God is showing us what Mr. Lincoln's war will be like. No home will be safe," he warned, his voice nearly drowned out by the wind and rain.

The guests abandoned the table for the parlor, where they sat quietly, exhausted by argument and waiting for the storm to abate.

Around midnight, several window panes blew out in rapid succession, and the Castle began croaking and wheezing, as if the building would fly apart in a million pieces. Water poured in through the empty windows, around the still-intact window panes, and through keyholes and doorframes.

The woman whose son had challenged John Ellsworth at dinner strode to the piano. She began with the hymns "Faith of Our Fathers" and "Crown Him with Many Thorns," but as more voices joined in and the tension eased, she picked up the tempo with "Oh! Susanna," "Listen to the Mockingbird," and "Row, Row, Row Your Boat."

They were in the middle of "Jeanie with the Light Brown Hair," when the gale quit abruptly, as if a huge door had slammed shut.

Relieved, the guests streamed out to the veranda just as the moon broke through the clouds and lit up the landscape. The lawn was littered with shattered glass, shingles, bricks, broken roof tiles, an entire window frame, and even a wagon wheel. The lone tree on the Castle property, a silver spruce that young Johnny had helped Ezra plant during that long-ago summer, had uprooted and fallen neatly into the narrow space between the main house and the barn, sparing both.

It took Ezra a moment to make out the pealing of a bell from afar. With his spyglass, he could make out a three-masted coastal schooner breaking up in Squimset Harbor, near the Seal Rocks. He might have heard people yelling and screaming as well, but he couldn't be sure.

The widow appeared at his side. "They need you more than we do."

Ezra was already on the shore path when the moon disappeared again, spigot-like rain began, and the wind picked up from the opposite direction. He'd only read about Caribbean hurricanes before, and now he was in one.

Rescuers had already piled driftwood into a mammoth pile on the beach and doused it with kerosene, and in spite of the rain, they were able to get a bonfire going.

The surf made it impossible to launch one rescue boat, so the dozens of citizens crowding the beach could only hold on to each other in order to remain standing and to comfort one another. They sang hymns for the victims they couldn't reach.

The bonfire survived the night, but not a living soul made it ashore.

The day dawned peacefully. The wreck had disappeared, but flotsam was scattered as far as the eye could see. Baled cargo bobbed innocently offshore. Black Rock Wharf, alive with arriving and departing vessels only hours before, had vanished.

The first body washed ashore at sunrise.

It was a young sailor, his eyes agape in horror and his open mouth filled with sand. Other crewmen soon followed, many in pairs and some alone—a pitiful sight. One, miraculously, still had his sailor's cap pulled down tightly over his eyes. The captain washed in alone, looking regal with the stripes on his epaulettes and the brass buttons of his uniform gleaming as if polished for the occasion.

They went about the grim task of bringing the bodies to the upper beach, where a small grove of evergreens that had survived the storm could protect them from the sun. The town's constable, who, like Ezra, was veteran of previous wrecks, stood watch for robbers. Meanwhile, the undertaker laid the victims out in rows that reminded Ezra of cots in the Georgetown barracks of his army days.

Two score and six bodies had been tended to by the time Ezra retraced his steps along the shore to reach the winding path to the Castle. A few yards beyond the cut in the shoreline marking the path, a subtle movement caught his eye.

In one of the numerous crevasses on that part of Egg Rock, another body had washed in on the rising tide. It was that of a young woman. She wore what Ezra guessed to be an ankle-length blue gingham frock. It had been ballooned by the tide up to her knees, and he wanted to ease it back to her ankles, where it belonged. One shoe was missing, and a scallop-bordered length of green kelp garlanded her golden hair. Over her, a redheaded man knelt on the overhanging rock, lifting her slender arm. Instead of chivalrously kissing her hand or proposing marriage, he was twisting a bejeweled ring from her finger. When he sensed Ezra taking in the scene, he dropped the lifeless limb, turned, and ran.

Ezra located a search party checking the shoreline nearby and led them to her. One of the men pointed to an object floating just seaward of the crevasse and, with a long stick, guided it gently to shore. It was a little girl no more than three, dressed in the same blue gingham as the woman.

"At least she found her mum," the man said softly.

It was nearly noon when Ezra finally got away.

He found the widow standing alone on the veranda. She was wearing an apron over her evening, not her morning, black dress. Like everyone in Egg Rock, she'd witnessed shipwrecks before, but he was shocked at how she'd aged overnight.

She had news. John had suddenly left for Boston. Without Ezra available to take him, he'd hired a neighbor for the trip to Squimset in his horse cart. He'd been so unnerved by the shipwreck that he could not bear spending another hour in accursed Egg Rock.

"I told him the road to Squimset might be blocked," she continued. "Do you know what he said?"

Ezra shrugged.

"'If we get stuck, I'll walk the rest of the way to the depot. If the tide is up, I'll wade across. The trunk can come later.'"

The widow turned to take a long look toward Squimset.

Ezra changed into dry clothes. Before going back downstairs, he trained his spyglass on the Rocks. A dozen or so seals were frolicking in the afternoon sun as if nothing out of the ordinary had taken place.

The Widow Ellsworth was at the kitchen sink, shelling peas. "He went down to the beach this morning, Ezra."

"Nancy, sit here with me. I have something to tell you."

She listened to his story about John and the drowned woman. "Do you remember the last time he came home?"

"How could I not? It was my first summer working here."

"A schoolteacher from Worcester came to tell me that her engagement ring was missing. We were on the way to her room to have another look, when we passed Johnny on the stairs."

She tugged at her apron, trying to smooth it out. "He said hello, but he looked past us, as if addressing someone else. When the two of you went to the beach later that morning, I searched his room. He'd hidden the teacher's ring in a shoe under his bed."

"Just before he jumped on the boat to Boston?"

She lowered her eyes. "He looked past me the same way when he got back from the beach this morning."

She sighed and, for the first time ever, rested her head on Ezra's shoulder.

# SHORE LEAVE

Seth Tarbox landed the lighthouse keeper's job on Egg Rock because he'd worked for the winning presidential candidate in 1884.
He was a political appointee but not a hack. He had never been a lighthouse keeper before, of course, but he was an experienced sailor who knew Egg Rock's waters as well as anyone.

His most vivid childhood memory was of seeing huge bonfires on the Forty Steps cliffs guiding survivors of a shipwreck to shore. After that wreck, in which dozens of men were lost, the Egg Rock lighthouse had been built to warn mariners away from nearby shoals.

He could have drawn a detailed map of the island's rocky shore from memory by the time he joined the Union Navy at seventeen.

They immediately sent him south, where he served as topman on ships blockading Confederate ports. After the war, he became first mate on a coal carrier between Halifax and Boston—until it broke up off Cape Ann during a snowstorm.

By then, he'd had enough excitement and good luck to last a lifetime, so he returned to Egg Rock; started fishing cod for a living; proposed to Alice Whitney, a girl he'd known since grade school; and settled down.

After all he'd packed into his life, it was hard to believe Seth was only twenty-five the day he got married.

Mr. Murdock, the keeper he'd replace, was certainly qualified too, but that was the way things were, and Seth wasn't going to lose sleep over one more of life's many injustices.

The telegram announcing his appointment arrived a week or so after the election. That gave them plenty of time to get ready, since they wouldn't be leaving the town of Egg Rock for the rock of Egg Rock, as Alice liked to say, until the inauguration in March.

Alice was excited about their adventure, but Ben, their eleven-year-old, had been so unhappy over the prospect of living on "that forsaken rock" that he'd convinced himself that Grover Cleveland would lose, Senator Blaine would be the new president, and Mr. Murdock would stay put.

They promised Ben that he'd be able to get to school in the spring and fall, but when winter came in, often with a fierce November gale, they could be marooned for months.

Murdock invited Seth out to the rock to learn the ropes while the weather held. He followed Murdock around to learn the routine and familiarized himself with the three-acre mound where he and his family would spend at least the next four years.

They spent most of those hours up top with the oil-fired lamp surrounded by an astounding array of beveled glass lenses. Murdock handled the equipment with a priestly attitude of awe and respect, but it was punishing work. The lamp consumed kerosene like, as Murdock put it, a ravenous dog, while the wick needed trimming every night, and the lenses, as handsome as they were, were the devil to keep free of soot. He kept repeating that only pristine lenses would do, or ships would miss Egg Rock Light's steady red signal and crash into the shoals and ledges nearby.

"You're lucky, son," Murdock confided, "because whale oil used to be the only fuel available. Nasty stuff. Smelled like dead fish and burned ten times dirtier."

Downstairs, Murdock's wife, Tabitha, had created a cozy home. A wide doorway connected the kitchen and sitting room on the ground floor, creating a single space that was filled with sunlight all day long. Framed pictures of sailing ships and lighthouses covered the walls, and the windows were fitted with gingham tie-back curtains.

At nearly six feet, Seth felt his hair brush the ceiling whenever he stood on tiptoe.

*A home for midgets*, he thought.

The Tarbox family moved in on Inauguration Day, March 4, 1885. The Murdocks insisted on spending their last night in the guest room, a closet-sized space with barely room for a bed. Seth and Alice took over the other bedroom, while Ben and his dog, Milo, slept downstairs in the parlor.

Murdock insisted on manning the tower with Seth throughout the night. It wasn't clear if it was because he was checking on Seth's ability to manage the equipment or because he craved the company. Anyway, by the time the supply boat came in the morning, bringing firewood, water, food, and dozens of barrels of kerosene, and the Murdocks loaded their things on board for the return trip, there were plenty of hugs and handshakes.

The Murdocks' parting gifts were Lucy, their nanny goat, and a butter churn. Seth watched as the boat approached the opposite shore, wondering how hard it would be for Murdock and his wife to readjust to a world they'd left seven years earlier.

Ben attended school in town until summer vacation. He boarded at the minister's home, where Reverend MacDonald's grandson Cyril, also eleven, already lived. A fisherman from town ferried the boy back and forth on Monday morning and Friday evening, weather permitting.

After the last frost in April, they planted a vegetable garden on a flat area just outside the kitchen. There were stories about how rich the soil was, but they were taken aback at how fast everything grew. They harvested string beans, peas, cukes, and summer squash in late June and their first root vegetables by August. Whatever they couldn't eat on the spot, Alice packed in glass jars and stored for winter.

As the days got longer, life got easier. Fewer hours were needed to maintain the lamp, making for quicker wick trimming and less time polishing the lenses. Father and son hauled fewer barrels of kerosene from the shed on the far side of the rock and up the spiral stairway to keep the light burning.

But Seth hadn't forgotten Murdock's last words to him as the older man helped Tabitha onto their boat back to the world: "Spend summer preparing for winter."

Ben's job was to slap a coat of paint on everything exposed to the elements, while Seth caulked the window frames and cemented obvious gaps between the building's granite blocks.

Milo adjusted to his new surroundings by learning to run back and forth, precariously close to the edges of the rock, chasing seagulls.

The dog was such a strong swimmer that Seth worried he'd try to swim to shore while Ben attended school, but Milo only went as far as an occasional fishing boat nearby. As a reward the men would throw him a couple of codfish tied to a stick.

Visitors were a welcome diversion. Alice's cousins, her only other family, sailed out from North Squimset one sparkling Sunday afternoon. Townsfolk came by, often leaving newspapers and magazines so the family could catch up with civilization. Once in a while, total strangers would show up just to see what a lighthouse keeper's life was like.

It was a happy time. On summer evenings, they sat outside to watch the gaslights flicker on one by one along Egg Rock Road—so close that they could almost reach out and touch them.

Alice always kept her almanac open on the kitchen table. At breakfast, she'd announce the times for sunset and the following morning's sunrise, since the lighting and extinguishing of the lamp were events around which each day revolved.

She made sure Ben saw moonrises and moonsets and the morning and evening stars, and as summer went along, she taught the boy all she knew about her favorite constellations. She pointed out details while he looked at the sky through an ancient pair of opera glasses that once belonged to Alice's grandmother.

For days before an expected eclipse of the moon, she fretted about the weather. When the day of the event dawned murky and cloudy, she was inconsolable. But her prayers were answered when, with minutes to spare, a brisk west wind kicked in, and the clouds lifted.

Before they knew it, Ben was back at school, Big and Little Egg Rock came alive with a patchwork of October reds and yellows, and the days shortened ominously. When the first nor'easter of the season struck in November, Ben gave up any thought of getting back to town. On the following Monday, an open steam launch, the last supply boat of the season, announced itself with clanging of its bell as it emerged from the fog.

After a week of unseasonable cold, fingers of ice began to form around the rock. The following morning, the fingers had lengthened and connected to form a giant spiderweb of white floating on the dark water. By the next day, the rock was fully encased.

The winter of 1885-1886 turned out to be the harshest in Boston's recorded history. It was impossible to keep the house warm, especially when the wind was up, and the elements had no trouble seeping through gaps Seth had missed between the ground floor's granite blocks.

Seth kept the light going without a moment's interruption from dusk to dawn. On clear nights, they could see ships passing to their east, out of danger, and when visibility dropped, Ben was put in charge of ringing the fog bell.

After Christmas, the thermometer never made it out of the teens. The kerosene thickened, turning the tedious task of filling the lamp into an hour-long marathon. A massive sheet of ice covered the water in all directions. The sky turned an unnatural deep blue by day, as if a landscape painter had chosen the wrong color, while the night sky was packed from zenith to horizon with brilliant stars.

Pewter-colored plumes of chimney smoke across the bay appeared frozen solid in midair.

Alice brought Lucy, the she-goat, inside and fashioned a bed for her next to the stove. Milo, everyone's friend, greeted her, tail wagging.

One morning, Ben awoke to find a giant icicle hanging from the rafters over his bed, and another crack in the roof had opened up over the spiral staircase.

Alice insisted on working the light after Seth spent two sleepless nights during a storm. Climbing down the spiral staircase at dawn, she slipped on ice that had formed there and bounced all the way to the bottom. Her screams awakened Seth, who found her crumpled on the kitchen floor with the splintered end of one tibia protruding through her long wool stocking.

The next six days were a nightmare for Seth and Ben, trapped in a sea of ice, helpless, while Alice Tarbox lay dying.

They carried her to bed. Seth was able to wash the wound with soap and water, coax the bone back in under the skin, and apply a splint they fashioned from a sawed-off mop handle and a bandage made from torn strips of bedsheet.

Fever began on the second day, and by the fourth, Alice slept fitfully, awakening now and then and conversing with people she imagined were in the room, including her long-dead grandmother. When her leg swelled, Seth took the bandage down to find the wound filled with awful-smelling pus.

At dawn on the sixth day, Alice stirred and opened her eyes. Her voice was weak, but her words were clear.

"Dear husband, when I'm gone, put me in the red taffeta frock, the one you love so much. And promise that before long you will find a new wife—and a new mother for our son."

She fell into a deep sleep and stopped breathing during the afternoon while sunshine was still lighting up the room.

Once they'd said their goodbyes, it was time for Seth to light the lamp upstairs and for Ben to stoke the stove for supper.

After his son went to bed, Seth carried out Alice's request. Between trips upstairs to refill the lamp and trim the wick, he washed her body and dressed her.

At first light, before Ben awoke, he carried Alice to the oil shed and laid her on the stone floor. The thermometer outside the kitchen door read three above—so cold that each breath made his chest burn.

Trying not to think of how appalling it was to abandon her like this, he rushed back to the house, lay flat on the kitchen floor, and wept.

By the time the boy appeared, red-eyed and pale, Seth had breakfast on the table.

They remained marooned on the rock for six more weeks, marking one year on the calendar while they waited.

They had sufficient food but only because Alice was no longer alive. Their fresh water was nearly gone, when a late-February snow came to their rescue.

Seth constructed a coffin with oak two-by-eights intended for a new kitchen table. He found a measure of comfort in covering its surface with whittled vines bursting with roses, Alice's favorite flower. He applied two coats of white paint, as if the box would be holding a child, since it was the only color he had.

Years later, Ben, by then a world-famous astronomer and a grandfather many times over, would recall those awful weeks for a man writing a book about New England lighthouses.

"I don't think Pa and I ever cried after that first day. We both loved my mother more than anyone else in the world, but we were too busy to mourn. Just keeping the light burning in the tower and trying to stay alive took everything we had. For most folks faced with such a loss, time stands still. I guess we were lucky that those days flew by the way they did."

At dawn on the first ice-free day, they began their journey. Even so, the time for lighting the lamp again was barely eleven hours away. They lashed the coffin, shimmering in the half light, to the back of the rowboat. Shoving off, they noticed ice floes, like miniature icebergs, drifting along farther out to sea.

Onshore, townsfolk gathered at Short Beach as soon as someone spotted Seth's boat. It had been a record four months since the supply boat had left its last cargo of the season in November, and the town's only contact with the Tarbox family since then had been the reassuring red glow from the lighthouse every night.

On the beach, a small band played, and people cheered—until the coffin came into view, and it became clear that Alice Whitney Tarbox hadn't made it through the winter.

Men rushed forward to pull the boat up onto the beach, while the rest stood back in respectful silence.

They placed the coffin on a wagon, and the group, with Seth

and Ben up front, followed on foot. Meanwhile, someone took off at a gallop to inform Reverend MacDonald.

The cortege grew block by block, and by the time they'd reached the Village Church, there were enough mourners to fill the pews. The minister began by reading a short scripture passage. Then he stepped down from the pulpit, removed his glasses, and spoke directly to the congregation. Quietly, so everyone had to lean forward to catch every word, he reminded them that he had married Seth and Alice and christened Benjamin right where he was standing. He went on to say that Alice had been in a terrible accident, and he left it at that. Finally, while Seth sat with his head in his hands, the reverend asked them to keep Alice's small family in their prayers. After the Lord's Prayer, the ceremony, which had lasted barely a quarter hour, was over. Burial, everyone knew, would have to wait until the ground thawed.

People stopped to express their condolences and then drifted off to resume their lives. Cyril and Ben went outside.

MacDonald was pouring two generous glasses of brandy when Seth walked into the library, and in no time, they eased into the type of free-wheeling conversation only old friends could have.

They reminisced about Alice, the girl whose mother had died in childbirth and who'd wanted so much to be a mother herself. They laughed when the minister recalled their wedding day, when the soon-to-be groom, shoes untied, had tripped over the threshold to make a grand entrance.

Outside, Ben and Cyril were letting off steam, tossing a ball, joking, and laughing.

"Good to hear that," Seth said, and instead of getting tearful, as MacDonald feared he would, he smiled the broad, gap-toothed smile that the minister had wondered if he'd ever see again.

"Did you catch sight of Kathleen Johnson?"

"Yes, in the back of the church. Where's Pete?" Seth waited while the minister closed his eyes, seeming to gather his thoughts.

"How could you know, trapped on that wretched rock all winter? Pete was thrown from his horse Christmas morning and broke his neck. Never knew what hit him. What about calling on Kathleen before going back? We'll watch Ben."

The Johnson house wasn't far, but when Seth set out from the church, the sun was already in the western sky. He and Ben still needed to order supplies, make it back to the beach, and row out to the lighthouse by dusk.

He'd grown up with Pete Johnson, who'd replaced his father in keeping the church building and grounds in order, digging graves, and maintaining the town's small cemetery. He couldn't imagine how the reverend was doing without him.

Kathleen had moved to Egg Rock while Seth was sailing on coal carriers out of Halifax. Her mother, Mrs. Steele, had lost her husband at Shiloh and had come to Egg Rock to be near his family. After the reverend's wife passed away, Kathleen began helping out at the rectory.

Kathleen and her mother were in the parlor when Seth pulled the bell. Even in deep mourning, Seth could see that Kathleen Johnson was a handsome woman.

A hired girl brought out a pot of tea and little cakes on a tray.

Seth did most of the talking. He told them about life out on Egg Rock and how Alice had referred to it as "Egg Rock the rock" instead of "Egg Rock the town."

Kathleen managed to smile, but Mrs. Steele sat straight-backed alongside, her jaw set and her eyes wary. She reminded Seth of a ship's mascot, ready to pounce on a rat or pursue an intruder.

"Yes," Kathleen replied when asked if she knew Ben. "He's a sweet boy."

Years at sea had made Seth Tarbox a disciplined man. "Look before you leap, and think before you speak" was how one ship's captain once had counseled him.

But the words tumbled out of him unrehearsed.

He needed a strong, healthy woman to be his new wife and a mother for his child. He expected to be the lighthouse keeper for at least another three years, possibly longer. Life out on Egg Rock could be hard, especially in winter, but in return, he could promise a comfortable home, an upright husband, and a good-natured son.

In the awkward silence that followed, he pulled out his pocket watch and got to his feet. Kathleen walked him to the door while her mother remained fixed to her spot on the settee. He imagined her eyes boring into him as he reached the door.

At Clara's General Store, Seth placed an order for delivery on the next day's supply boat. Meanwhile, he bought a leg of lamb, a pound of potatoes, a jug of cider, and a cherry pie for their first real dinner in months. He added the latest copies of the *Boston Transcript* and *McClure's Magazine* to the pile on the counter, while Ben got a bag of licorice and a copy of the book he'd heard so much about, *Huckleberry Finn*.

They shoved off from Short Beach with a good two hours to spare. While Seth rowed, Ben rested his head on one of the packages and dozed off.

*My dear son*, Seth thought. *I see so much of Alice in you. What was I thinking, speaking to Pete's wife like that?*

Seth had only a half barrel of kerosene left, so at dawn, it was a relief to see the sun coming up over a flat sea.

He looked up from his chores every few minutes to see if the two-master had rounded Forty Steps on its way from the town wharf.

When there was no sign of it by noon, Ben joined his father outside. He'd picked up the opera glasses from their accustomed spot on the kitchen table.

"To bring us luck," the boy responded to Seth's quizzical look.

As if on cue, the boat came into view, and Ben handed his father the glasses.

The reverend and Cyril were leaning over the bow to get the best view, while Kathleen Johnson stood behind them in the prettiest blue dress.

"I'd best put on my clean shirt!"

Seth soon reappeared in what Alice had always called his "wedding suit." His shoes were laced and tied, but he was still fixing his cravat.

By then, there was no need for opera glasses.

"Well, I'll be damned" was all he could say.

As a rule, the supply boat needed only thirty minutes to deliver provisions, water, firewood, and the all-important kerosene and take on the scores of empty kerosene barrels for the trip back to shore.

However, for this special occasion, it stayed for twice that long. The passengers disembarked with the reverend in the lead, taking Kathleen Johnson by the arm.

Seth was dumbfounded by the transformation. Kathleen, who'd looked so closed up and uttered barely a dozen words the day before, looked like the happiest woman alive. He was comforted in knowing that Kathleen's mother had family in Egg Rock and would not be alone.

A moment later, Cyril stepped onto the small dock, turned, and held out his hand as he helped Mother Steele off the rocking boat.

Cyril smiled warmly, but the old lady marched past Seth without a glance.

The reverend strode to the center of the parlor, drew a small book from his pocket, and motioned the couple forward.

The entire wedding party consisted of six humans and one dog.

The instant Seth and Kathleen finished exchanging their "I do's," the boat's bell clanged loudly, and the wedding party dispersed.

After a minute alone together, the newlyweds walked outside to wave goodbye to their guests.

In the meantime, Mother Steele had navigated the spiral staircase—and was already picking out her bedroom.

# *F*ORTY STEPS

My name is Homer Lowe. Dr. Quimby, the warden here at the Danvers Lunatic Asylum, has ordered me to write down my autobiography in order to facilitate my treatment. Since I have spent my life as a poet and a professional letter writer, he says I'm a special case.

I am permitted to write only on days when the voices quiet down enough for me to think clearly. The warden told me not to allow my mind to wander far afield but, rather, to concentrate on matters that seem germane to my condition.

My only request was to get my typewriter brought out here since my penmanship, once so impressive, is now nearly unreadable.

I was born in Egg Rock to a family who had been among its

earliest settlers. My great-grandfather raised dairy cattle out there, and when he tired of making the trip over the sandbar to and from Squimset every day, he built a cottage near Bear Pond for his family.

I grew up as the middle child of five. The only thing that set me apart from the others was my keen interest in writing. By that, I mean the physical part of it. I loved penmanship, and as long as I can remember, I've had a sharpened pencil with me so I could jot down words the way some kids love to draw. As I grew older, I became interested in books. I was no prodigy, but I was among the first of my schoolmates to read.

For years, I worked for a book bindery in Squimset. The owner, a sweet gentleman by the name of Ingalls, had deep respect for the old volumes that came to his attention, and he taught all of us who worked for him that we were privileged to be preserving history, like medieval monks. Many books from colonial times came into the shop since we were known for our meticulous care of ancient texts. Mr. Ingalls saw great potential in me, he said, and he taught me everything he knew about the business. Until I got sick, he expected me to run the business myself one day.

While working at the bindery, I began writing poems and hearing voices that no one else heard. I could not tell if the voices brought about the poems or if it was the other way around, but they all started at about the same time.

My first published poem, "Castle Rock," appeared on page three of the *Squimset Sentinel* a week after my twenty-second birthday. I loved seeing my own words in print, but the greatest thrill was finding my poem next to "Seal Rocks" by Henry Wadsworth Longfellow. A *petrous pairing*, I thought at the time. Perhaps I too would become a famous poet one day.

The publication of my poem lifted my spirits. Even my father, who had little patience for books or poems, congratulated me, expressing the hope that I could actually make money from the scratching of a pen. Best of all, the dreadful voices quieted down.

I wrote Longfellow a letter, telling him how much I loved his work, especially "Evangeline" and "Paul Revere's Ride," and how proud I was to have my poem printed next to his own. Days and weeks went by while I awaited the response that never came. My admiration for the man eroded as months went by, replaced by disappointment and anger.

I encountered Longfellow one day while walking along the shore near Forty Steps. I tipped my hat as he passed, but he kept walking without any acknowledgment of my greeting.

The news of Longfellow's death weeks later upset me but not in the way I would have expected. My mind latched on to the absurd notion that my thoughts had killed him.

My first breakdown came without warning soon thereafter, on a lovely spring morning. Mr. Ingalls had the windows thrown open to air out the big workroom. The birds seemed to feel that it was a festive occasion and serenaded us from the nearby trees. However, the voices inside my head soon hijacked their song.

I was working on the most valuable book ever entrusted to me: a slim volume of Anne Bradstreet's poems printed in 1678. I was repairing its fractured binding with needle and thread.

The woman I most feared took over, drowning out the others. Her voice was the most innocent sounding but the most frightening of all. *Mellifluous* is the best word I could ever find to describe it. She knew how to use honeyed language that made me think the most awful thoughts.

"Prick your finger with that needle, and bloody the pages," she wheedled.

I succeeded in smearing only the frontispiece before Mr. Ingalls restrained me. I'm sure he was angry, but I remember most vividly his eyes filling with tears.

That was how I made my first trip to the Danvers Lunatic Asylum and had my first encounter with Dr. Phineas Quimby. When I arrived, I was most unhappy. I paced my cell at all hours, was unable to sleep, and refused to eat. For this agitated state, the doctor ordered an intense regimen of hydrotherapy. Seven days a week, I spent four to six hours up to my neck in a large tub of steaming water. After a month went by, my condition stabilized, and Dr. Quimby allowed me to join other inmates for walks around the leafy grounds surrounding the complex of Gothic-appearing turreted buildings. But soon I became lethargic, barely able to leave my cot. For that, the doctor ordered a second round of hydrotherapy, only this time, with ice baths and cold compresses. The seesawing water treatments continued for almost two years, until my condition stabilized enough for me to be discharged back to my home in Egg Rock.

On the day of my departure from Danvers, Dr. Quimby wrote out two prescriptions: "a vigorous daily walk for at least two hours every day in salubrious salt air, rain or shine" and "one minim of belladonna *q hora somni*," to aid my digestion. Days after I got home, Mr. Ingalls came by to visit. In spite of my terrible act of vandalism, he continued to take a fatherly interest in me. He had even made the trip out to Danvers to visit me over Christmas. This time, he had a new job for me, if I was inclined to take it.

Mr. Ingalls's cousin Jenny was married to Lydia Pinkham's son. Most people know who Mrs. Pinkham was, but in case a reader of this document does not, she was an entrepreneur, probably the most successful businesswoman in the country, and by far the wealthiest woman in Squimset. She made her fortune by creating Lydia E. Pinkham's Vegetable Compound, whose secret ingredients were promoted as a cure for a variety of women's ailments.

I agreed to meet Jenny Pinkham the following day. The job was to reply to customers who were urged in advertisements to write to Mrs. Pinkham directly for advice. Since Mrs. Pinkham was deceased, I'd be writing the letters. When formally offered the position, I jumped at the opportunity. I would make twice my bookbinder's salary, and I would be able to work from home, which would give me time to carry out Dr. Quimby's exercise regimen.

It was odd that I, a thirty-year-old bachelor, would be offered such an assignment, but I never gave voice to my doubts. My writing skills apparently outweighed other considerations.

The younger Mrs. Pinkham gave me copies of letters her mother-in-law had written and suggested I use them as a basis for my correspondence. She stressed that the letters should be as personalized as possible. She detested the idea of form letters that looked as if they had rolled off a penny press, she said. Finally, she gave me a brand-new Remington No. 2 typewriter for my work.

Just as Dr. Quimby had predicted, my medical condition remained stable for a few years. I'm convinced my daily walks along the water played a role, but spending each morning at the Remington while crafting a handful of personal letters gave me an outlet for creative energy that I sorely needed.

In the beginning, one annoying detail troubled me: the Remington's capital letter *I* had a distinct forty-five-degree fissure on its vertical. I tried cleaning the key and even resorted to inking over the defect before finally concluding that no one besides me would ever notice it.

As a finishing touch, I signed the name Mrs. Pinkham with ornate flourishes and addressed each envelope in calligraphy. Adding those touches to each correspondence took more hours than coming up with original words for the text, but the exercise kept my mind occupied with something other than itself.

I did feel awkward offering guidance about menstrual irregularities, cramps, discharge, and so forth, but soon it became routine. At times, I needed to contact Jenny Pinkham for advice. I often received questions about the alcohol content of the compound, and she advised me to reassure the customer that an infinitesimal amount of alcohol was added as a "solvent and preservative agent."

The voices never went completely away, but for nearly five years, they remained on the periphery of my consciousness. One day, without warning, they became full-throated again, forcing me to wear earmuffs not only in the winter but all year long. I'd been known as the town eccentric for years, so my appearance in earmuffs on the shore path in the middle of July caused no stir.

It took a while for me to realize that I was also seeing things. My mother, who'd been dead for many years, appeared in the kitchen, standing in front of the stove. At other times, however, I couldn't decide whether I was experiencing a hallucination or seeing something real.

One unusually raw summer afternoon, I took a long walk—with my earmuffs firmly in place—because the voices were screaming at me. The woman who had made me smear Anne Bradstreet's verse with my own blood so long before was leading the chorus again.

"You must get back to the task at hand," she insisted.

I made a total circuit of Big Egg Rock that day, more than twice my usual distance. By the time I reached Forty Steps, the voices had finally quieted down. I marched down the wooden staircase, counting each step out loud, as I was accustomed to doing. Afterward, I sat on the beach to rest and took in the view of Castle Rock and Egg Rock beyond, topped by its granite lighthouse.

Just then, when things seemed so peaceful, I had the most horrible vision of my life. A boy or a small man stood motionless on one of Castle Rock's outcroppings with a fishing pole in hand.

I moved behind a large boulder so I could observe him without distracting him. Then I saw a much taller figure approach the fisherman from behind and strike him on the head, sending him, with the pole still in his grip, tumbling to the ocean below.

The following day, I learned that the minister's son had gone fishing and failed to return home. The day after that, the town was abuzz with the terrible news that the boy's body had been found washed up at Forty Steps.

I was afraid of going to the police because I still could not tell how much of what I'd seen had come from inside my own head.

Besides, who would believe anything that Egg Rock's resident lunatic reported?

I got much sicker after that. Mother stood in the kitchen for hours each day, and I'd see Mr. Longfellow walking with friends at Bear Pond, the Black Mine, and Forty Steps. Still, every time I encountered him and tipped my hat, Longfellow looked right through me as if I didn't exist.

As for the voices, I kept earmuffs in place all day and night and stuffed cotton into my ears, but the voices were louder than ever.

By the end of the year, I was back at Danvers. Dr. Quimby, as kind and as dedicated as ever, started me on a treatment he'd been experimenting with, called hypnosis. Improvement came but slowly. Four years would pass before I could go home again.

My letter-writing job was gone, but I soon learned that it was for the best. An article appeared in the *Ladies' Home Journal* that rocked the Lydia Pinkham empire. A photograph of Mrs. Pinkham's gravestone appeared with the caption "Who is writing Lydia Pinkham's 'personal' letters?"

There was one letter that I finally had the strength to compose—to the Egg Rock chief of police. In a few lines, I described the moment when I'd witnessed the minister's son's murder. I steeled myself for the inevitable interrogation at the police station, but no one ever contacted me.

I started writing poems again and submitted dozens to every newspaper and magazine I could think of. Finally, the *Squimset Sentinel*, publisher of my first poem nearly twenty years earlier, ran my "Ode to the Lighthouse Keeper," again on page three.

Walking became a problem because of recurring flares of gout that kept me homebound for weeks at a time.

Once the voices started keeping me up all night, I knew I had to do something, or I'd be sent back to Danvers. That was when the idea came that I could perform my own hydrotherapy. Desperate, I limped to Forty Steps one November morning and dove in. The water was so cold that it burned my skin, but I stayed with water up to my neck for several minutes. As I exited the water, shaking uncontrollably, Mr. Longfellow and his friends appeared. Instead of looking through me, however, he pointed his long, bony forefinger in my direction, and they all laughed as if they'd never seen anything so ridiculous in their lives.

I spent the day wrapped in blankets in front of the stove, and it was growing dark before I could feel my hands and feet again. After supper, I put a pile of rags, a small jug of kerosene, and a dozen wooden matches in a sack and waited until midnight, when the shore path to the Longfellow house was sure to be deserted.

The lights were out when I arrived. I soaked the rags, placed them in separate piles under the veranda, and struck the matches. In minutes, the house was engulfed in flames. I'd planned to take off for home right away, but the fire was so beautiful and gave off such welcome heat that I couldn't move.

I was standing next to the adjacent boathouse when the fire brigade pulled onto the property, and within the hour, I was in a straitjacket, sitting in a wagon on the road to Danvers.

It took months of treatment before I could understand that the Longfellow house was empty that night, boarded up for the season, and remember that the poet had been dead for fourteen years.

I realize that I'll be serving a life sentence here. With no hope of release, I've written this document only to please Dr. Quimby, who has been so kind to me.

# $\mathcal{B}$OTTOMS UP

Climbing the spiral staircase in the dark, Ben recalled the time his daughter, Alice, had said, "Papa, nighttime is your favorite time of day."

Now Alice, a mother herself, was asleep downstairs while Ben tiptoed his way up to the widow's walk.

There had to be a couple dozen of them in Egg Rock—square wooden platforms atop houses' pitched roofs. It was sad to imagine a woman standing up there and praying for the safe return of a husband's ship already at the bottom of the sea.

Ben's wife detested the term *widow's walk.* "Lugubrious," she called it. She referred to it instead as the belvedere. In any case, Phoebe never ventured up there.

Years before, he'd glassed in the widow's walk and installed a refracting telescope with the widest aperture available. Phoebe was uneasy about it. The house, built for her great-grandfather nearly a hundred years earlier, was a family heirloom, and the ancestral portraits that lined the walls of the hall downstairs were a daily reminder that she was now the custodian. The mere thought of defacing Whitecaps was, as she'd once cried out in a moment of pique, like drawing a mustache on Grandmamma.

But she needn't have worried since no one seemed to notice the alteration. Or if they did, they were so proud of the professor that they were willing to overlook it.

Phoebe didn't understand the technical aspects of astronomy. The scraps of paper covered with mathematical formulas scattered all over the house might as well have been Sanskrit love letters, she remarked to a friend. But if a visitor inquired about her husband's work, she could go on and on about his pioneering telescopic photographs, his ideas about galaxies speeding away at the speed of light, and how he, the great Benjamin Tarbox, had succeeded in verifying Einstein's theory of relativity.

Unlike her, Ben was a townie whose family had lived in Egg Rock for generations. The Appletons were summer people, prosperous Bostonians who escaped to their cottages in Egg Rock to sail, swim, and socialize away from the city's heat every year.

Ben and Phoebe had met as teenagers, and with willful ignorance, they'd violated the unwritten rule that the summer people were to keep to themselves, as if a bright red line had been drawn around their properties on East Point.

In the early years of their marriage, summers at Egg Rock were awkward, with whispers about *that* couple. But fame came early, and with it came not only acceptance but adulation.

Now the day the professor arrived for the season was an annual Egg Rock event, nearly as big as Christmas and the Fourth of July.

Ben had been worrying about the weather all week, just as he always did when a big celestial event was on the calendar. This time it looked like he was in luck; an afternoon thunderstorm had cleared the air, setting the stage for a perfect sunset and a sparkling June night.

As much as he loved sunspots, the Crab Nebula, and planetary transits, eclipses were his all-time favorite events.

He was most intrigued by total solar eclipses and had spent much of his professional life chasing them. Unlike any other celestial event, a total solar covered only a tiny sliver of the earth's surface. Since his student days, he'd made three long voyages to view total eclipses: to Spain in 1905, Brazil in 1912, and Principe, an island off the west coast of Africa, in 1919. In Spain, the sun was fuzzy on account of persistent fog, but Brazil was far worse. Already clouded out, the scientists got soaked by torrential rains while they huddled outside, hoping for a miracle.

However, Principe made up for the others. With more than six minutes of totality in the clearest sky imaginable, the eclipse was as memorable as Ben's wedding day and the days each of his children were born—all rolled into one.

His work at Principe, with empirical proof that starlight was bent by the sun's gravity, just as Einstein had predicted, catapulted Benjamin Tarbox from a highly respected scientist to a household name.

"From a big fish in a small pond to a very big fish in a very big pond" was the way Phoebe put it. She might have added that her husband was a rather cold fish as well, but she kept that opinion mostly to herself.

The spiral staircase was like the one at the Egg Rock Lighthouse, which had become Ben's family home when he was eleven. There, his mother had taught him everything she knew about the night sky, and he'd observed his first lunar eclipse through her ancient pair of opera glasses.

The day the Smithsonian honored him for "making the heavens more accessible to all of us," he donated those opera glasses to its permanent collection.

Before getting the telescope ready, he made a leisurely survey of the world spread below him. Whitecaps sat atop the highest rise in Egg Rock, and with three high-ceilinged floors below him, the widow's walk commanded a 360-degree view.

Boston's skyline took up a hunk of the western horizon, with only a fraction of its lights aglow at two in the morning.

The lighthouses were going about their silent work, punctuating the darkness with their signatures. The Boston, with a single flash every ten seconds, guarded the Inner Harbor. The Graves, with two flashes every twelve seconds, was the brightest as it watched over the Outer Harbor only a couple of miles from where he stood. But Ben's favorite, whose beacon his mother had pointed out from atop their own lighthouse decades earlier, was Minot Ledge Light, some dozen miles to the southeast. According to an ancient Indian legend, Hobomock lived deep in the ledges from which he unleashed frightful storms. Mother believed the Minot's signature—one-four-three with two seconds between the flashes, followed by five seconds of darkness before repeating—was a perfect antidote for that evil spirit.

"You see, dear, it spells 'I love you.'"

He could barely make out the abandoned Longfellow property nearby, while at the bottom of the hill, the old Fremont cottage hugged the shore, dusky in the moonlight. Turning east, he caught a glimpse of Castle Rock towering over Forty Steps.

Egg Rock crouched like a watchdog offshore. Its lighthouse, where Seth Tarbox had been the keeper for twelve years, had been decommissioned, abandoned, and finally demolished. No trace of its existence remained.

Looking out a window over a sleeping town or sitting in an observatory while calibrating his instruments always made Ben feel as if he had the whole universe to himself. That sensation of being king of the hill, as Phoebe had once called it when he'd tried to explain, he knew, was the real reason he'd become an astronomer.

The spell was broken when he noticed a pulse of red light no more than a half second in duration just off Castle Rock. He counted out loud, hoping for it to repeat itself, and was rewarded with an identical pulse twenty-five seconds later.

That was followed by a flash of light from shore, and through binoculars, he could see a pair of open-topped automobiles parked off Egg Rock Road and pointed toward the water. Focusing on where he'd seen the red pulse, he could make out a small vessel with the typical high bow and low, flattened stern of a lobster boat.

F. X. Mulcahy, usually the most confident of men, felt his

knees shaking. The rendezvous with the rum ship, a converted submarine chaser, had gone smoothly, with a half dozen silent guys—"Frenchies," he'd been told—loading two hundred cases of Canadian whiskey onto his deck in ten minutes flat. He passed the twelve-mile limit without interference and saw no sign of the coast guard all the way home. Even when Egg Rock declared itself with a string of flickering streetlights and all reason told him he'd made it, he couldn't stop shaking.

Just off Forty Steps, he signaled, waited half a minute, and repeated. His second signal was immediately met with a flash from shore, and he steered the *Connemara* southeast for the last leg of his trip: around the tip of East Point to the drop-off location on the old Longfellow property.

Two fancy roadsters were waiting, and one turned on its headlights as he docked. Again, silent men made quick work of unloading his cargo, and after getting a handshake and a wad of bills from a gentleman in a fashionably cut suit and a boutonniere, he eased the *Connemara* away.

Only then did he notice the darkness. On his way back from the rum ship, the moonlit ocean had made him less anxious than he might otherwise have been, but now, in the home stretch, the sea was black. He looked up to see the moon in eclipse and wondered if it was an omen.

"Never again," he muttered aloud as he cut the engine and inched into his space at the town wharf.

The eclipse had begun, but Ben was drawn to the drama playing out below. He switched from binoculars to his scanning telescope and followed the lobster boat as it rounded East Point. Meanwhile, the automobiles headed across East Point, and with lights out and practically on top of each other, they swung onto the Longfellow property. Signals were exchanged like before, and as soon as the boat pulled in, boxes were loaded into the vehicles, which exited the property and sped toward the causeway to the mainland.

Keeping an eye on his pocket watch, Ben clocked the whole affair at forty-one minutes.

But the police never appeared.

He turned his attention to the darkening moon, but by then, he was too angry to concentrate. Hands shaking, he lost his grip on the scanning scope, and it hit the floor with a crash, shattering the objective.

Too exhausted to navigate the spiral staircase, he stayed put and waited for dawn. In the meantime, he tried to figure out what had made him so furious.

Rum-running was an open secret, of course, and he had his share of illegally purchased spirits in the wine cellar downstairs.

But Egg Rock was a special place for him, a kind of Eden. The world and all its problems belonged at the other end of the causeway, and he'd do everything in his power to keep things that way.

Watching diamond-bright Venus rise out of the ocean just before dawn, he realized that the night, nearly the shortest on the calendar, had been the longest of his life.

His first order of business, he already knew, would be to deal with the police.

---

The station was quiet when Ben walked in. Part of the small structure, he'd once heard, had been Egg Rock's original one-room schoolhouse. The only other time he'd been there had been to report lights left on in a cottage after a family had left for the season.

The young officer at the desk greeted him warmly. "What can I do for you, Professor?"

The cops he'd known growing up all knew him as Ben, but they were long gone. The young fellow seemed starstruck.

"Chief Cooper should be here any minute. You're welcome to wait in his office."

The chief arrived minutes later, in a dark blue uniform with one gleaming star on each shoulder. Phoebe and her friends called him Egg Rock's most eligible bachelor.

He shook Ben's hand, sat behind his desk, and waited for him to speak.

Ben gave the chief a detailed report of what he'd seen and ended with a question. "Did the police know anything about this?"

"Not to my knowledge, Professor. Have you shared this with anyone else, including your wife?"

"Not yet."

"Let's keep it that way. You'll hear from me soon."

After supper, Chief Cooper pulled up in front of Whitecaps and rang the bell. Ben noticed him eyeing the Appleton family portraits as they walked the long hallway to his study at the back of the house.

Waving off the offered seat, the chief got right down to business. "I brought along an item I need you to read but not touch." He unfolded a sheet of paper, smoothed it out, and set it on the desk.

It was a typewritten statement. The signature at the bottom had been covered.

> I witnessed the murder of Cyril MacDonald on Castle Rock in the town of Egg Rock, Massachusetts, on June 13, 1889.

Cooper stood silently while Ben slowly read and reread the document, committing every word to memory. Once he stood back, Cooper slipped it into an inside pocket.

The chief spoke again, slowly, delivering each word with the precision of an expert marksman. "Last night you saw an eclipse, Professor—nothing else."

Cooper made his way out of Whitecaps alone, while Ben, suddenly light-headed, dropped into the nearest chair.

Sitting there, he tried to recall every detail of what he'd just read.

The page was professionally typed, with no typos. The only abnormality was the capital *I*. Midway along its vertical was a distinct forty-five-degree fissure sloping downward from left to right. It was present all five times the letter appeared.

Concentrating on such a meaningless detail was a dodge, he knew, but gave him time to settle down.

The three-paragraph statement contained information that Ben had never shared with anyone.

Cyril and Ben had been best friends growing up. During the first years that Ben's father manned the lighthouse, he boarded with the MacDonald family while attending school. They were both bright, curious boys who were comfortable with each other.

But as they grew older, they developed different interests. Ben read everything the library could find on planets, stars, comets, and galaxies, already working toward his goal of becoming an astronomer. Meanwhile, Cyril became more involved in Egg Rock's Village Church, where his father was minister. Physically, Cyril never seemed to grow, while Ben shot up nearly a foot in a year.

Ben became an athlete, while Cyril's favorite pastime was fishing.

Although Cyril was also a year-rounder, he had more in common with the summer people than Ben did. It was socially acceptable to be the son of a clergyman, especially one who ministered to the summer people, rather than the son of a lowly lighthouse keeper. As they approached their midteens and social occasions took on more significance, they found themselves in two different worlds.

There was also the matter of Phoebe Appleton. Ben had taken a shine to her, and she always seemed to enjoy his company.

However, when she arrived for the season the summer they both turned fifteen, she informed Ben that she would no longer be seeing him because Cyril was her new best friend.

Ben was hurt, of course, but was wise enough to understand that being turned down by a girl wasn't the end of the world. Besides, he was too busy to dwell on it. He had a dream job that summer, tending the lawns and gardens at one of Egg Rock's grandest summer cottages near Forty Steps. He made the first real wage of his life and shared a hearty lunch with the staff at noon each day. By the end of the summer, he'd be able to buy his first telescope—and would gain a desperately needed ten pounds.

He was weeding the vegetable garden one afternoon, when he spied Cyril carrying a fishing rod over his shoulder. Ben wanted to say hello, but Cyril never looked in his direction as he passed the house and crossed the road for Castle Rock. The day had turned windy and raw, and as far as he could see, Forty Steps and Castle Rock were deserted.

After work, Ben walked out to Castle Rock with the idea of saying hello. But when he saw his old friend standing all alone on an outcropping, rod in hand, he knew he hated Cyril MacDonald more than anyone else on the face of the earth.

At breakfast, Phoebe seemed to be waiting for Ben to mention Chief Cooper's visit, but when he didn't bring the matter up, neither did she. He announced that he'd be going back to the college to take care of a broken telescope lens and another problem that needed attention. She nodded her understanding, as she always did when it came to his professional life.

"Try to get back for the Dory Club Dance on Saturday" was all she asked.

"We'll see."

He boarded an express train out of South Station and watched the western suburbs roll by and dwindle to farmland. Then he closed his eyes and concentrated on his mental photograph of Cooper's document.

> A slightly built boy holding a fishing rod stood on a spit of rock over the ocean some hundred feet out from Forty Steps. He caught my eye because it was such a peaceful scene. Suddenly, a much taller boy walked up behind him and struck him on the head with something, perhaps a large rock. Immediately, the boy who had been fishing tumbled headfirst into the ocean below.

Ben hadn't shed a tear since the day his mother died. When their first child was stillborn, Phoebe was inconsolable, but he'd soldiered on, dry-eyed.

He made it to the washroom at the end of the car just in time. Standing at the sink, he watched his reflection in the mirror as tears streamed down his face.

Then he confessed, saying the words out loud for the first time in his life.

"I noticed a good-sized boulder at my feet and considered its appearance propitious. My hands were shaking with rage, but I still managed to hold it steady while I sneaked up on my old friend. 'Howdy, Cyril!' I was pleased that my voice sounded so matter-of-fact.

"He turned and smiled at me just before the rock struck him full force."

The news was splashed on the front pages of newspapers all over the world:

> Ben Tarbox, America's Astronomer, Dead at 53, Body
> Found Seated at Telescope in College Observatory;
> Apoplexy Suspected

Chief Cooper drove out to Whitecaps to inform the professor's wife in person. The chief put on a convincing performance, looking shocked and grief-stricken.

So did Phoebe Appleton Tarbox.

Of course, neither knew then that the other one was acting.

# ⟋⟍ PICTURE IS WORTH A
# GAZILLION WORDS

Dennis Tierney never had trouble
sleeping. Ever since he'd gotten
sick, he could drop off seconds
after hitting the pillow, sleep for
eight hours straight, and be out of
bed by six in the morning. On the
rare morning he overslept, he felt
as if he'd done something wrong.

That was what made the night
so unusual.

"Anticipation," he muttered to himself. He'd kept himself busy
in the darkroom until after midnight, and he finally closed his eyes
around half past four, just as it began to get light outside. But matters

could have been worse. If he hadn't telephoned his brother, Tom, he wouldn't have slept at all.

Tom had seemed surprised by the call, since Dennis never asked for anything. Yes, he'd said, he understood why Dennis was reluctant to navigate the roads alone on Egg Rock's biggest day ever, and sure, he'd be happy to help out. He'd agreed to come by at noon, just when the wedding ceremony was scheduled to begin at the Village Church on East Point. That way, he'd have plenty of time to push Dennis up Ocean Street to the Egg Rock Club before it got too crowded.

Dennis had been counting the days since he'd learned that the groom's father, who happened to be the president of the United States, was expected. He also understood that plans could change at the last minute with the world acting so crazy. He'd heard on the radio that Japan had bombed Canton, and Hitler was about to invade Czechoslovakia, so he was relieved to learn that FDR had spent the night before the wedding on a coast guard cutter anchored only a mile off the town wharf.

This would be his second encounter with FDR. Years before, Dennis had been lucky enough to get invited to Warm Springs, Georgia, for what they called "rehabilitation"—paid in full by the March of Dimes. The future president had arrived the same day.

Roosevelt obviously loved it there, spending hours with the other patients at calisthenics, in the pool, and for lunch, with his wheelchair pulled up to one of the long tables in the dining hall. When he'd learned that Dennis was from Egg Rock, he mentioned that he'd enjoyed visiting the town while he was in college and looked forward to seeing "that enchanted isle" again someday.

"And I'll be looking for you when I do."

Now that FDR was in the White House, Dennis wasn't so sure about that. Advisers made sure the president never looked disabled. No pictures were permitted of him in a wheelchair, on crutches, or being helped around. Hobnobbing with other cripples the way he did at Warm Springs was out of the question.

The braces were Dennis's first challenge of the day. He'd start by rolling to the edge of the bed, grabbing the bar attached to the headboard, and pulling himself to a sitting position. After lacing them as tightly as possible around his skin-and-bone legs, he'd stand, pivot ninety degrees, and settle into his high-backed wheelchair.

Next was the trip to the bathroom, where he'd pivot out of the chair onto the commode, wash, shave, brush his teeth, and, finally, get into his clothes.

His father had studied his son's predicament the way he approached any other engineering problem. By the time he died, Dennis Senior's innovations—the extra-low hospital bed; strategically placed grab bars; widened doorways; lowered sinks, counters, and light switches; ramps; and even a small elevator—had transformed the Tierney family's Victorian to a laboratory dedicated to making Dennis's daily life tolerable and giving him the independence he craved. His final project, started when he was well into his seventies, had been to widen and lower windows so that Dennis, in his chair, could see as much of the outside world as anyone else. Father, never at a loss for words, had called that innovation his "aesthetic contribution."

Dennis called it his crowning achievement.

Yet in those first nightmarish days of his illness, his father had been the least understanding member of the family. Perhaps, Dennis concluded, he'd created this engineering marvel to make amends.

It all started on a perfect summer day. Dennis had turned eighteen the week before and was headed to college in the fall. Life could not have been sweeter.

He was with his girlfriend, Rosemary; his brother, Tom; and a couple of other kids, diving off the back of their boat at Forty Steps.

The blue-black water at Forty Steps was, except for Bear Pond, the coldest in Egg Rock, but on that August afternoon, it was perfection.

After a few dives, he thought he'd twisted his back, but he was having too much fun to pay attention.

On the way back to the wharf, his legs tightened up so much that he had trouble getting out of the boat. That night he had a violent chill, and his mother piled on blankets like it was the middle of winter. Soon he was burning up and had the worst headache of his life. Mother picked up the phone to call Dr. Kendrick, when his father stepped in.

"It's just a summer bug, Mary. He'll be fine in the morning."

But when Dennis Tierney needed to use the bathroom around dawn, he couldn't get out of bed.

His father was irate, claiming Dennis wasn't trying. It took days for him to pipe down and see what was really going on, but when he did, he became his son's fiercest advocate.

Dennis was lucky to have come away paralyzed only from the waist down. Eleven-year-old Willy Steele came down with infantile paralysis the same week. He was rushed to a hospital in Boston, where he died a few days later. People said that Willy had the worst kind of polio, called bulbar, which cut off swallowing and then breathing. Willy had been swimming too. His sister and brother had to carry him home from the little beach near Bear Pond.

After that, people assumed that all the beaches were infected with the polio germ. The authorities closed them down, posting blood red signs with the word *WARNING* in big block letters and a skull and cross-bones underneath.

Anyone who ventured into the water was arrested.

Tom arrived at the Ocean Street house at the appointed time, and it took only minutes for him to push his brother's wheelchair up the hill to the Egg Rock Club. Notices plastered on lampposts all over town and in the window of Clara's grocery store announced that a reception for the family would be held inside, but all townspeople were invited to festivities on the lawn, featuring a band concert and refreshments.

Just as they reached the gate, Egg Rock's lone police car pulled in. Chief Cooper, in a snazzy new uniform with a single silver star on each shoulder, eased his tall frame out of the driver's seat and joined a group of men in dark suits.

"Secret Service," Tom volunteered.

Vinnie and Walter Mulcahy were standing by the front door, ready to wait on tables inside. Dennis was impressed at how the starched white shirts, bow ties, and haircuts made these scrappy boys look almost respectable. Vinnie spied the camera on Dennis's lap.

"You should get some great shots from over there," he said, pointing to a spot under an ancient copper beech.

Dennis settled in, checked the settings on his new Leica, and watched the scene unfold.

He'd never taken a single picture before getting sick, but that changed when his aunt Margaret gave him her late husband's Graflex Speed Graphic as a get-well gift. Bud Tierney, who Dennis had never seen without a cigar jammed in his mouth, worked the night shift for one of the Boston papers, specializing in crime scenes.

The Graflex was a giant compared to the camera now on his lap, but it was classy, with a polished oak frame and brass fittings. In those first weeks when Dennis was bedbound and terrified, the Graflex had kept him from going insane.

Father had written a letter to Dartmouth College, requesting that they delay his admission on account of illness. A year later, Dennis had written a letter himself, forfeiting his place. By then, he knew he'd never be an engineer.

Instead, photography became Dennis Tierney's field of study and his passion.

Dennis Senior had approached a colleague and amateur photographer for advice on building a darkroom, and Paul Bickford had come by to look at the old butler's pantry off the kitchen to see how it could be converted.

Dennis and Paul Bickford had hit it off, and before long, Paul became a regular at the Ocean Street house. Once the darkroom had been built, he'd stocked it with the essentials: chemicals, trays, a contact printer, and a primitive enlarger.

He'd then turned to Dennis. "Okay, kiddo, are you ready to learn?"

He hadn't needed to ask twice.

Dennis had quickly adjusted to navigating the room, barely illuminated by the red safelight. Soon he'd learned to flip film from a camera, process it into negatives in a small tank filled with developing solution, and dry the negatives on a tiny clothesline with the tiniest clothespins imaginable. Lessons on printing and enlarging had come next, culminating in the best moment of all, when he held the photographic paper under the surface in the developer tray and watched the final image appear.

Only then had Paul started teaching Dennis the ABCs of picture taking. The technical stuff, such as f-stop, shutter speed, focal distance, depth of field, was just another form of engineering after all. Days before taking his first portrait—of his friend Paul in his Sunday best—he'd learned how to change lenses in seconds, and before his first landscape—of Bear Pond at sunrise—he had mastered the basics of judging depth of field and calculating white balance.

The dining room had become his studio. A tripod sat at one end of the room for portraits; chairs and settees for his subjects to sit on and interchangeable backdrops, rolled up like window shades, took up the opposite end.

Dennis's father had devised hand controls for his old Plymouth coupe, allowing him to travel around town. Soon he'd been taking school pictures and covering weddings at the Village Church.

More than anything else, the little hand-controlled coupe gave him mobility. Cruising out to Forty Steps, if he didn't look down at his legs, he could pretend he was cured. Forty Steps, the place where his illness had begun, became his favorite subject—and he never lost sight of the irony. Over the years, he would amass a collection of photographs of the beach, with its terraced staircase; Castle Rock, with its mysterious outcroppings and recesses; and Egg Rock itself, jutting out of the ocean a quarter mile offshore.

Forty Steps beckoned him at dawn, at dusk, in the moonlight, on foggy mornings, during thunderstorms, after a snowfall, on the hottest summer afternoons, and in the dead of winter. It had become his private research station, where he experimented with telephoto lenses, fish-eye shots, filters, super-light-sensitive film, and color.

Years later, after being forced to abandon Egg Rock forever, Dennis would conclude that Forty Steps, like his father, had been given a chance to atone for its earlier actions.

Dennis often wondered how he would have ended up without Aunt Margaret, who had brought the old Graflex to his sickroom; Dennis Senior, who had engineered his independence; or Paul Bickford, who had taught him the skills and self-confidence he needed to reenter the world.

Townspeople were soon streaming onto the grounds of the Egg Rock Club, which was dominated by one of Egg Rock's oldest buildings. Built by a man who'd made a fortune selling ice all around the world, its facade of rough-hewn granite blocks reminded Dennis of its old nickname: the Igloo.

The bride and groom arrived in a closed sedan behind three police motorcycles in a V formation, followed by an open convertible carrying the president, Eleanor, and an old lady the Mulcahy boys said was the president's mother.

FDR's hair had thinned, and his face was fuller than Dennis recalled. His eyes were ringed with dark circles, as if he hadn't slept in days, but he seemed energized by the crowd.

FDR motioned Dennis to come over, rotating his hands as if they were the wheels of Dennis's chair.

"You were in Warm Springs!" It was a statement, not a question. His voice was unmistakable, with the high-pitched, aristocratic singsong rhythm Dennis remembered.

"It was 1928, sir, from New Year's until the middle of March. You have an incredible memory."

"It comes in handy for this line of work. Show my son how that contraption works. He's not the one getting married today, so he should have time to take a picture or two."

It turned out to be three.

Two attendants lifted FDR out of the car. As they carried him into the club with his legs slack and his feet inches off the ground, the president gave Dennis a conspiratorial wink. "On to the Igloo!" he joked as he glided past Dennis's chair.

Townspeople shook Dennis's hand and tousled his hair. The band was launching into "Yankee Doodle Dandy," and Tom offered him a tall glass of beer.

He shook his head. "Let's go."

Although he couldn't put it into words just then, he knew they had to get the hell home before his luck ran out.

Ocean Street was deserted. About halfway home, Dennis pointed to the empty garage at the McBrien house. They had sold the family car after Mr. McBrien died a couple of years earlier, and Dennis had seen Mrs. McBrien at the reception.

"Push me in there."

Inside, the garage smelled like dead flies and crank-case oil. The walls were covered with dozens of old license plates neatly nailed in long rows. The Leica people claimed you could change their film in full light, but Dennis wasn't taking chances. Once Tom had closed the doors, Dennis clicked the film beyond the last exposure, removed the old roll, pocketed it, and inserted a fresh roll in its place. Finally, he adjusted the Leica's focal length to infinity and selected the longest shutter speed before clicking off a dozen new shots of a blank wall barely visible in the half light.

The police car was parked in front of the Tierney house when they came around the bend at the end of the street. Chief Cooper was accompanied by one of the men Dennis had seen at the wedding reception.

Cooper greeted them warmly, as if he'd just stopped by to shoot the breeze. Then his tone changed.

"It's about your pictures, Dennis. We will need to examine the film—for security purposes."

The other man nodded in agreement.

Dennis went through the motions, acting puzzled and reluctant before finally giving in. "Security," he knew, was baloney. Newspapers were already running pictures of the preparations for the big day in Egg Rock. Photos and newsreels of the president at his son's wedding were sure to follow.

"We'll have the camera back to you in a day or two," the chief added, as if addressing an obstinate child. Then he turned the ignition and drove off.

Once Tom left, Dennis peeled off his braces and stretched out on the bed. The next thing he knew, a dream awakened him. It was already getting dark outside when he opened his eyes.

*I'm crossing a wide, bumpy road in my wheelchair. An open car comes into view with FDR, Eleanor, and the president's mother in the back seat. I wave my arms frantically to get the driver's attention, but the car keeps bearing down on me. I try to yell, but my mouth is too dry for me to make a sound. Just before impact, I catch sight of silver stars on the driver's shoulders.*

Around midnight, he developed the film and cut it into negatives, which he hung on the line to dry until morning. Too keyed up to lie down again, he spent the rest of the night in his chair, listening. Whenever the house settled or the wind rustled leaves in the trees, he pictured Secret Service agents, their fedoras pulled low, surrounding the house.

Gabbro, his old Maine coon cat, spent the night on patrol,

padding from room to room and circling back to check on Dennis every once in a while.

At dawn, Dennis wheeled himself back into the darkroom to make the prints.

Holding the paper in the developing pan, he thought of a bunch of things that could go wrong. Maybe he'd chosen the incorrect aperture setting, maybe the president's son didn't have a steady hand, or maybe one of them had blinked.

But he wasn't disappointed.

The first showed Dennis in his chair and the president at the open door of the convertible, shaking hands. In the second, both men were smiling like old friends as they looked directly at the camera. But the last shot captured the moment best. With a far-off look on his face, FDR was holding his hand above Dennis's head like a priest giving a silent benediction.

Later in the week he found the camera—minus the film—at the bottom of his mailbox. There was no note and no more visits from Chief Cooper.

That left the matter of the pictures.

He considered hiding them in the strongbox kept under the cellar stairs, burying them in the vegetable garden, or even dousing them with lighter fluid and watching them go up in flames.

He telephoned Paul Bickford for advice, and before he knew it, he was giving Paul the okay to call the editor of the *Squimset Sentinel.*

They sent a reporter over that afternoon and in the next day's city edition, the picture of the president giving Dennis his blessing nearly filled the front page under a seventy-two-point headline: "Egg Rock Man and FDR Meet Again."

Dennis settled back into his accustomed routine, but since it was wedding season, that meant working day and night.

One afternoon, the postman rang the bell instead of leaving the mail in the box.

"I saw the return address and thought you'd want to see this right away."

It was a large envelope from the White House, Washington. Inside was an eight-by-ten glossy of the benediction picture with a handwritten inscription: "To my friend and fellow survivor, Dennis Tierney, FDR."

Dennis ordered the nicest gold-trimmed frame he could find and hung the glossy in the parlor for all the world to see.

For weeks, townspeople showed up to have a look. By the time things finally got back to normal, just about every Egg Rocker had visited.

It was getting late when Dennis finally made it home. He'd spent the afternoon at Forty Steps, trying to get the perfect shot of a grove of peak-colored maples on the beach's north cliff.

Wheeling up the ramp, he saw Gabbro sitting in the last small patch of sun near the door, patiently licking his paws.

*Someone had let him out.*

Dennis already knew what he'd find, or rather not find, by the time he reached the parlor.

The Benediction was gone.

# $\mathcal{T}$HE CURLEW BEACH INCIDENT

"Who the heck was Curlew?"

That was the first question Priscilla Crane asked when she heard about the house on Curlew Beach.

Her friend Gretchen shook her head, laughing.

"Oh no, my dear, there was never a Mister Curlew! Curlews are birds. I expected that a writer like you would know

that! Legend has it that curlews used the beach as a way station on their migrations between Canada and the tropics. But they're gone now."

Gretchen seemed to know so much about so many things, and curlews were no exception. She also knew just about everyone, including a woman who was leaving the Boston area until the war was over and wanted to rent out her house. When Priscilla mentioned that she needed to find a secluded place to write, Gretchen snapped her fingers and—presto!—made the introduction.

The place was just what Priscilla was looking for. It sat on a point of land in the little town of Egg Rock with a fine view of Boston.

The woman was anxious to take her young son back to family in Kansas now that her husband had been shipped off to England.

Since Priscilla was equally anxious to get out of the city, things moved fast.

She and Bing moved into the house in June, the week after D-Day. The one-year lease would be renewable for the duration of the war. Unlike the cottages nearby, the house was fully winterized.

Stepping onto the veranda, she took in the beauty of her new surroundings and made a wish.

*To spend the rest of my life here in this paradise.*

A bright-eyed old lady dropped by later. "I'm from up there, in the summer anyway" was how she introduced herself, pointing to a big house topped by an impressive widow's walk.

Bing, who never barked, wagged his tail in greeting.

"Doesn't look like much of a watchdog to me," she continued, furrowing her brow. "You know, it can get pretty lonely out here, especially after Labor Day."

It took Priscilla all summer to get her bearings. At first glance, Egg Rock looked like the sleepiest town imaginable, about as far from the real world as one could get. But that was an illusion.

It was an open secret that German U-boats prowled offshore, so the peninsula, stretching into Boston's Outer Harbor from the north, had become crucial to the city's defense. Military installations, with conning towers and gun emplacements, housed enough men to triple the town's prewar population.

Clara's General Store in the town center was a reminder of simpler times. Clara stocked just about everything, from canned goods to homemade pies, flyswatters, and comic books. If she didn't have something in stock and it was legal, she'd have it brought over the causeway from Squimset. If Squimset didn't have it, she'd order it from Boston. Essential items were rationed, and Clara, seated behind the cash register all day long, double-checked the ration stamps before ringing up each order.

The same went for gasoline. Mr. Ward could fix a flat, replace a spark plug, or change the oil. However, with gasoline so scarce, Priscilla only drove her Chevy around the island to keep the battery charged.

The town library would not have been out of place in Down East Maine, but Miss Pettigrew, the librarian, operated much like Clara at the market. If she didn't have a book Priscilla needed, she'd borrow it from another library.

War or no war, Priscilla had landed in a writer's nirvana.

None of this would have been possible without her father's trust fund.

She was brought up in Back Bay in a mansion full of servants. It was an idyllic childhood, with summers on Nantucket, governesses, dancing lessons, and cotillions. But her life changed the day her little brother drowned in an ice-skating accident when she was eleven. Her mother—pretty, sociable, and loving—took to her room right after the funeral and rarely emerged. Her father, already a successful businessman, would be gone for weeks at a time.

Priscilla's center of gravity soon moved from the Beacon Street brownstone to school, where she wrote for the student newspaper and made friends.

It seemed predestined that her father would collapse on a train returning from New York and that her mother wouldn't awaken from an overdose of barbiturates a week later.

At age seventeen, six weeks shy of graduation, she was officially an orphan.

Gretchen, an orphan herself, never let Priscilla out of her sight during that dreadful spring.

"My guardian angel," Priscilla called her.

She and Gretchen, who had already shown a talent for drawing, both landed jobs at McRae, Boston's only advertising agency. The positions were for stenographers—the only job other than housekeeping that a woman could get at McRae.

Priscilla did her share of typing and shorthand but was soon writing radio ads on the side. Her jingle for the Jordan Marsh department store won her a handsome under-the-table bonus, but everyone understood the system.

Women copywriters didn't exist. Only their work did.

She soon learned that getting the reader's or listener's attention was the be-all and end-all of advertising. The job was to pull them in and hawk the product, and then you were done.

But that wasn't enough for her.

She intended to write stories that people would remember long after putting down the book. Hooking the reader, she realized, was only the first step in a complicated process.

Priscilla didn't need the money, but McRae gave her life structure. It allowed her to escape the cavernous Beacon Street house each morning, fall into an office routine, and write.

She was given additional work on the side, and before long, she was a full-fledged copywriter (except for the title), cranking out more ads than any of her colleagues.

Her thirtieth birthday came and went, and with it came full control of her trust fund. Priscilla knew she was at a crossroads. McRae's president had hinted at a big promotion, but she pictured herself turning into another one of those ladies she'd encounter on the subway: stooped gray-haired women dutifully making their way to offices downtown. It was a trap ready to be sprung.

If she didn't become a full-time writer now, she never would.

The first step would be selling the Crane home and moving away. The city, she was convinced, was too distracting for a serious writer.

Gretchen had once asked her what kind of serious writing she'd be doing.

"I'll know once I settle down and start thinking."

"With all those radio jingles, I thought you'd be a poet."

She was trying to decide how to proceed, when Guardian Angel Gretchen dropped by and told her about the house at Curlew Beach.

The house could have been custom built for her. It stood out from the stately Victorians nearby, looking molded into the landscape instead of towering over it. Its huge floor-to-ceiling windows and wide veranda took full advantage of its setting.

The views from inside were equally spectacular, but every inch of wall space was covered by old pictures and maps. Bookcases were overflowing, closets were packed, and the attic was barely navigable. It seemed nothing had been thrown away during the hundred years since the house was built.

A pen-and-ink portrait of a formidable-looking woman filled the space above the parlor fireplace. Gretchen studied it carefully before standing on a chair and lowering the gilt-edge frame to the floor.

"Good luck!" she exclaimed when she examined the back. "See?"

In flowing script, with all sorts of curlicues and flourishes, was the inscription "Jessie Benton Fremont, 1868."

The next day, Priscilla asked Miss Pettigrew at the library if she'd ever heard of Jessie Benton Fremont.

"You're living in her house!" the librarian exclaimed. "Let me get you something from the stacks."

Minutes later she set down a pile of books. "Poor Jessie," she sighed, "so ahead of her time—and so forgotten! Ever heard of Kit Carson?"

"Sure."

"That's only because she wrote about him."

Jessie Benton's husband, John C. Fremont, known as the Pathfinder of the West, had been a general in the Mexican War, governor of California, and the first Republican candidate for president.

The Fremont books said little about Jessie directly, but as Priscilla read on, Jessie seemed to constantly hover in the background, just out of sight. Jessie had written stories for newspapers and magazines about the general's exploits—with Carson—and she managed his campaign for president and encouraged him to publicly oppose slavery.

Priscilla searched the clutter in vain for a diary since women of Jessie's position and era usually kept one. She did discover innumerable notes scribbled in the margins of books, newspaper clippings, letters, household accounts, and invoices.

That was when it dawned on Priscilla that she wasn't only renting a house for the duration of the war. She had also become the curator of the Jessie Benton Fremont Museum.

Right under her nose was enough raw material for a novel that could bring Jessie Fremont back to life.

Before she made it back to the library, she happened upon Miss Pettigrew at Clara's General Store, waiting for the butcher to finish with another customer.

She thanked the librarian for carrying those first books down from the stacks. "That's what got the ball rolling."

"You mean that you'll be writing about her?"

"I've started. And I already have a title: *Out of the Shadows*."

Miss Pettigrew, who up to then had looked like the perfect librarian from central casting, mousey and dour, broke into an honest-to-goodness grin. "Stand aside, Kit Carson!"

Gretchen was Priscilla's only regular visitor, lugging her easel, paints, and brushes to Curlew Beach. The water there reflected the light in unexpected ways, and the shoreline, ringed with birches and evergreens, transformed itself endlessly.

"Like Monet's haystacks," she'd proclaim with mock irritation, and then she'd add under her breath, "Dream on, girl!"

Some days she'd paint nonstop, but on others, she'd stand with brush in hand, waiting for the angle of the sun to change, a cloud to pass, or mist to rise to capture the right lighting.

On account of the blackout, however, she was always over the causeway to the mainland before sunset.

Egg Rock was blacked out every night, but not everyone took the order seriously. At Clara's, patrons joked about the air raid warden, an eccentric little lobsterman named F. X. Mulcahy. Apparently, the tiniest chink of light from a window would send him into a fury, and he'd threaten the violator with a night in the town's lockup.

But Clara went to his defense. "What if your two boys were out there fighting?"

The radio was Priscilla's most immediate link to the war. After D-Day, the tide seemed to turn, with the Japanese abandoning one Pacific Island after another and the Allies rolling into Paris.

Around town, there were whispers about the coast guard installing an electromagnetic harbor defense system to keep U-boats away.

As the summer wore on, people felt confident enough to imagine the Boston skyline aglow and the jewel-like lighthouses in the harbor flickering on again.

It was only a matter of time.

On Labor Day weekend, Priscilla's neighbors boarded up their cottages, packed up their cars, and left her to fend for herself.

The widow-walk lady rode by in a taxi, giving Priscilla a tentative wave goodbye.

Gretchen moved the large pen-and-ink portrait, positioning it so that Jessie Benton could oversee Priscilla's writing.

After taking Bing on his daily walk, she'd work until noon. On days when words came more easily, she wouldn't quit until her fingers cramped up or her eyes gave out. If an idea came to her in the night, she'd jump out of bed and jot it down.

She recalled what an older writer once had told her: "When all cylinders are firing, forget about the so-called necessities of life. Writing becomes the only necessity."

September and October flew by. At Thanksgiving, Priscilla had to settle for a capon from Clara's since no turkeys were available. Gretchen made the day more festive by bringing along an impossibly scarce bottle of Bordeaux red.

"Where did you get this?"

"Shhh!"

After dinner, Gretchen asked to see the old Longfellow place up the hill on the far side of the beach. Bing led the way with his nose to the ground. The only remnant of the burned-down house was an indentation in the ground, surrounded by field stones marking the cottage's dimensions.

Gretchen turned toward the boathouse nearby, the only structure that the fire had spared. She studied it carefully, reminding Priscilla of how she'd stand patiently before her easel, waiting for perfect light.

"I can see why this was so popular with rumrunners," she murmured.

A week later, Priscilla opened her door to a world blanketed in snow. She thought it must have been some terrible cosmic mistake to have winter come so early—until she realized that it was already December.

Along with the first snow, a mimeographed notice appeared under her door. Everybody knew about the Big Guns. They were built into hillsides south and west of Curlew Beach. Although details were supposed to be top secret, Clara's market buzzed with detailed descriptions of the two sixteen-inchers and two six-inchers poised to blow up enemy ships twenty miles out at sea. Everyone also knew that the conning towers were manned day and night, waiting for an enemy ship to be sighted.

"Our Christmas present" was the way Clara herself put it while seated squarely on her stool at the cashier's desk. According to the notice, the so-called test was scheduled for 10:00 a.m. on Christmas Eve.

People were advised to remove pictures and mirrors from walls; take glassware, china, and bric-a-brac down from shelves; and open all windows a crack to disperse vibration.

Still, Priscilla wasn't prepared for what happened.

Two nearly simultaneous booms hit her eardrums the way icy water once had when, acting on a dare, she'd taken too deep a dive in the ocean. The shock wave, a second later, nearly knocked her to the floor. The ground shook as if Egg Rock were having an earthquake, tossing the house around so violently that she pictured it slipping from its foundation and the roof coming down on her. Bing fled to the woodshed outside the kitchen and didn't reappear until the next morning.

Until then, Egg Rock had been her cocoon. The splendid house, the quiet beach, and a seemingly endless string of serene days when her only task was to pound away at her typewriter made the war seem as far away as Saturn.

But on Christmas Eve, the Big Guns brought the war home.

On those last days of the year, she couldn't write a word. She spent hours poring over newspapers in the library's reading room and kept the radio on late into the night. By then, the Battle of the Bulge was in full swing with German troops breaking through Allied defenses all over Belgium.

It was a tentative, uneasy Christmas for Priscilla and everyone else in Egg Rock.

New Year's morning dawned overcast, cold, and calm.

The little beach where those funny long-beaked birds once had nested formed a perfect arc that stood out sharply—white, black, white. Between the snow on the ground and the whiter-than-snow sea ice just offshore, Priscilla could make out a narrow dark strip of beach wiped clean by high tide. As the sky brightened, the birches along the shore came alive, and the evergreens farther back revealed themselves little by little.

Priscilla imagined Gretchen standing there with her brush in the air, waiting for the perfect moment.

She broke off her reverie and started up the hill to the Longfellow place, but Bing stayed behind. He tilted his head just like the dog on the phonograph record and, for the first time in his life, let out a ferocious bark.

The sound echoed along the empty beach and lingered for a moment in the trees before dying out. Beyond the sea ice, the water was dark and still in the half light. Following Bing's line of sight, Priscilla glimpsed a bright patch of water, as if the surface had been broken. Seconds later, the patch reappeared closer to land, and she could make out a long black object washing in with the tide.

She assumed something had fallen off a passing ship, until she understood.

There was a person out there!

The body raised its head and looked straight at her before dropping its head again, the way she and her brother would play dead man's float when they were kids.

She ran to the ice-rimmed shore, trying not to slip on the rocks underneath. When she reached the open water, the body was right in front of her. Digging her feet into the sand, she pulled it onto the beach.

By then, she was sure it was a man. He was about her height and wore a black rubberized suit and oversize aviator goggles. His lips, dusky blue in the growing daylight, were the only flesh she could make out.

Whoever he was, she needed to get him off the beach and into the house.

Carrying him was out of the question. She remembered the wheelbarrow leaning against the back wall of the garage. She'd used it the evening before to haul firewood into the house.

She told him to hang on and ran like hell while Bing stood guard next to the body.

He was still breathing, his eyes closed, when she got back.

"You need to be inside, where it's warm. If we can get you into the wheelbarrow, I'll push."

A hint of a smile crossed his face so fleetingly that she wasn't sure if she really saw it. He opened his eyes and struggled to his feet.

"If you steady me, we can walk together," he said matter-of-factly.

He had no accent. Maybe he was a soldier from a nearby base after all.

She draped a blanket over his shoulders, and like a drunkard and his wife, they staggered up to the house, where he collapsed into a chair.

She managed to strip off the rubber suit and soaked long underwear, put him on the sofa in the parlor, and piled on more blankets. He had no dog tags or insignia. There was a narrow leather bracelet on his left wrist but nothing else.

He was a fine-looking man who appeared to be about her age or a little younger. Although short and thin, he was muscular and fit. Priscilla was intrigued by the way his deep brown eyes offset his blond hair and pale skin.

She found a hot-water bottle and constantly refilled it from the kettle on the stove.

The thought of calling the authorities crossed her mind, but she decided to wait until morning. At dawn, she picked up the receiver but changed her mind again and put it back on the hook before the operator came on.

It was already too late.

He'd stopped shaking, but while he slept, he grunted and heaved his chest with every breath, as if he'd stop breathing altogether.

But he didn't die.

Over the next days, he opened his eyes briefly, studied the room, and took a few spoonfuls of soup before drifting off again.

It was a week before Priscilla could get him upstairs. Settled in the big bed, he spoke for the first time since New Year's morning.

His name was Jake Benz.

He was born, he said, in a small Pennsylvania town, the son of a German immigrant father and a second-generation immigrant mother. It was an unhappy home. With his father often out of work, they were forced to accept financial support from his in-laws.

A scholarship to a local college allowed him to escape, and when the American Olympic Committee visited campus, recruiting German-speaking students for their support staff at the Berlin Olympics, he was first in line.

He fell in love with Germany during that Olympic summer, and when it was time to board the ship home, he went missing.

*Oh my God*, she thought. *How could I be such a fool?*

"So you're a spy?"

"Yes, Priscilla, I can't deny it."

"I could turn you in."

"They'd ask questions, you know. I've been here a week."

He'd come by submarine. The U-boat had surfaced off Egg Rock, just outside the new harbor defenses. The plan had been to swim to the point of land south of Curlew Beach, on the old Longfellow property, but unexpected currents had forced him onto the beach itself.

Clothing, travel documents, and food had been hidden on the property. If he didn't claim them in twenty-four hours, they'd be taken away.

Soon he was strong enough to eat normally. Priscilla was lucky that the owners had left the cupboard well stocked with canned goods. She'd heard that extra ration stamps were available on the black market, but Clara, who had a nose for such matters, would have smelled a rat.

Was he homesick?

"Not for a minute," he replied, as if she'd asked a silly question.

She soon learned he'd left a life behind.

He'd found work teaching English in a town near Frankfurt. Before the war began, the foreign ministry had hired him as a translator, and he'd begun espionage training soon after. By then, he was married.

"Do you have anything to remember her by?"

He fixed his eyes on the wall above Priscilla's head. "Personal effects are forbidden."

She wondered about the leather bracelet on his left wrist but was afraid to ask.

He paced the upstairs rooms at all hours like a caged animal. Finally, he announced it was time to leave, but he worried he wouldn't get far without the proper clothing or papers.

She offered to check the Longfellow place in case the package had not been picked up. With an ironic half smile, he told her to look under the boathouse dock, where it would be tied to a crossbeam.

She and Bing found nothing, but on the way back, she devised a backup plan.

She pulled a blue serge suit from the back of a closet. The house's owner likely had left it behind since he'd have no use for it in wartime London or wherever he was going. She took the waistband in a few inches and shortened the sleeves and pant legs. After washing out some nasty grease stains and giving it a good pressing, she was satisfied.

She brought him a driver's license she'd seen in the desk downstairs.

"Excellent!" Jake said with rare emotion. "Bring up the typewriter, erasers, and a bottle of ink. I'll also need vinegar or rubbing alcohol. If they're not here, try Clara's."

He showed off his handiwork the next morning. The Kansas driver's license was now in the name of Jacob Benz of Topeka, with a birth date of April 28, 1916. He was five feet six inches tall, weighed 140 pounds, and had blond hair and brown eyes. The expiration date was April 1946.

"Ever met a Jayhawker before?" he drawled, sounding as if he'd just ambled out of a cornfield.

The day before getting on the road, he asked Priscilla for a haircut.

Good old Gretchen, the girl who knew everything, had taught her a little barbering when they were both at McRae. For a time, they'd done each other's hair.

Pairing her index and middle fingers as a guide, she started at the back of his head. Instead of being bristly like a man's beard, his hair was as silky as a woman's. Working her way back from the temples, she remembered to bend each ear away from the scissors the way Gretchen had shown her. Jake's ears were perfectly proportioned, with delicate shell-like whorls and a touch of pink along the edges.

This man who'd washed up in front of her house—this Nazi spy—was the most exquisite and terrifying human being she'd ever laid eyes on.

They remained silent as she continued her work.

As she made her way up to the crown, examining each tuft as she progressed, he let out a barely audible groan.

She finished off the top, evened out the front, and ended by tidying up the nape of his neck.

When she showed him the results in the mirror, he gave her his first genuine smile.

She was still gripping the scissors when he kissed her. She must have dropped them, but she had no memory of them clattering to the floor. Neither uttered a word while they removed each other's clothes.

The only other time she'd slept with a boy had been back in her advertising days, but she couldn't even remember his name. He was a friend of a friend, visiting from out of town, and he'd taken her by surprise. From start to finish, it couldn't have lasted ten minutes. Ten minutes after that, he was out the door.

She had no idea how long they made love. It could have been hours or only a few minutes, but they must have fallen asleep.

Loud banging at the door woke her. The ceiling light she'd turned on for the haircut was still burning, and since the blinds were up, she could see that it had grown dark.

In seconds, she was on the staircase, pulling on clothes.

"Open up!"

The door flew open as soon as she released the bolt. F. X. Mulcahy, the air raid warden, nearly knocked her over. He took the stairs two at a time and burst into the bedroom. On his heels, Priscilla was relieved to see the bed empty.

"You hidin' a boyfriend, missy?" He was an unremarkable man except for his icy blue eyes.

Just then, a car door slammed outside, and they heard heavy footfalls on the stairs.

"Mulcahy, you up there?"

Before the warden could answer, Chief Cooper was in the room, looking unhurried and professional. "Come with me," he said coolly.

The warden, flushed and shaking, followed.

Only when Priscilla heard the police car round the bend at the far end of her driveway could she take a breath.

She discovered Jake's body under a blanket in the bathtub. His lips, which had been so blue the morning he'd washed up on Curlew Beach, were cherry red. The mysterious leather bracelet lay on his chest, and when she caught the burnt-almond smell, the puzzle pieces fell into place.

Mulcahy, Cooper, or a platoon of marines could march in anytime, she knew, but she saw no choice but to get rid of the body.

She turned the taps on full blast, eased Jake's body to the surface, and slid him out of the end of the tub, sending him crashing to the floor. She dragged him by the arms down the stairs, through the kitchen, and out the back door. After bringing the wheelbarrow flush with the back landing, she slid him in and rolled him to the beach.

If she dumped the body in the ocean, it would inevitably wash back in—and the police would be sure to return with questions.

She was in luck. The moon was a few days past full, and the tide was out. If it was cold, she didn't feel it.

The sand was partially frozen, keeping the walls of Jake's grave from collapsing as she dug deeper.

She was in such a hurry that she gave little thought to the horror of what she was doing. Instead, she concentrated on the walls and stones she needed to remove. As the hole got deeper, she was pleased that she could no longer see the body, which lay on its back, filling the wheelbarrow.

Finally, she inched herself out of the hole and took one last look. His eyes were half closed, and his face was relaxed, as if he were taking a pleasant nap.

Tears of gratitude ran down her cheeks. If Jake hadn't poisoned himself, he'd have had no choice. Before leaving Egg Rock, he would have killed her.

Dropping the body into the grave and covering it up were the final steps. Big and little stones went in, making an audible thud as they struck his flesh. As exhausted as she was, she got a second wind as she flung the last shovels' worth of sand on top.

The moment she finished stamping the sand in place, the incoming tide flooded the gravesite.

It was past midnight when she rolled the wheelbarrow back to the shed, peeled off her clothes, and washed herself at the kitchen sink. After changing, she sat at the kitchen table and downed a generous dose of brandy in one ferocious swallow.

It took the rest of the night to scrub everything down, but by sunrise, she was able to walk out of her perfectly innocent-looking house for Bing's morning walk.

She spent the next nights in total darkness with the blinds drawn tightly, listening for the warden making his rounds.

But Mulcahy never came back.

On the third night, nature gave Priscilla another gift, as if the moonlight, the half-frozen ground, and the tide that had waited for her to finish her work hadn't been enough.

Two feet of snow filtered down on Curlew Beach, blanketing everything.

With her typewriter safely on the desk downstairs, she wrote more furiously than ever, completing the first draft of *Out of the Shadows* by the end of March.

Even when she missed her second period in a row and lived on Uneeda Biscuits and honey-laced tea to control the nausea, she kept on writing.

Priscilla couldn't remember the last time she'd climbed the ladder to the attic. The thought of going up there crossed her mind every time Jacob was about to show up, but she always found an excuse to put it off. Then she got too old to even consider it.

Well, now it was crunch time. Jacob and Katie were already in the air. She recalled how her father used to call her Priscilla the Procrastinator.

"Pretty damned good for eighty-nine," Jacob had said the last time he'd been in Egg Rock, over Christmas.

That was before Leo Mulcahy gave her the latest medical bulletin about her heart. One of the valves had narrowed down, allowing only a trickle of blood to get pumped into the circulation. He'd mentioned surgery, but she'd dismissed that with a wave of her hand.

Leo had given her one of his "Whatever you say" smiles. He'd been a prince the way he'd let Priscilla chart her own course for years, and this time would be no different. She'd be fine, he'd reassured her, as long as she didn't overexert herself physically or emotionally. First off, that meant no stairs. The next day, she had her bed brought down to the parlor and made the ground floor home.

She could control her physical activity to some extent, but putting a lid on her emotions would be trickier, especially with a big birthday to celebrate and her son coming home.

"What about writing?"

"That's just the point, Priscilla. I—and the rest of the world— want you to keep writing forever."

Temperamentally, no one could have confused Leo with F. X. Mulcahy, the air raid warden. Only one exceptional detail still rattled her after all these years: Dr. Leo Mulcahy had inherited his grandfather's piercing blue eyes.

Writing was on hold for now, with her birthday only a few days off. Besides, there had been no peace since the article appeared in the *New York Times*. Too bad, she thought, that you had to be pushing ninety with your ticker on probation to make the front page of the Book Review.

Priscilla Crane was, according to the article's last sentence, "a feminist trailblazer whose unwavering sense of justice permeates and elevates her work."

When the phone started ringing off the hook, she let the machine pick up the messages. Most were the usual congratulations, but one message stood out.

It came from a person she didn't know, a woman named Lotte Jones. She'd seen the *Times* piece and had a question: Did the name Jake Benz mean anything to her?

Priscilla immediately dialed the number, which had an area code she didn't recognize.

The woman answered with a cheery hello, but her voice seemed to cool when Priscilla introduced herself. Maybe she was having second thoughts.

But she popped the question again, and Priscilla answered, "Yes, a long time ago."

Lotte thanked her and fell silent. Priscilla thought the line had gone dead before the woman spoke again.

"Would you mind answering a simple question? Then we'll know if we're talking about the same person."

"I need to hear the question before agreeing to answer."

"Fair enough. When did you meet Jake Benz?"

"January the first, 1945."

Again, there was silence on the other end, and Priscilla worried the woman had hung up for real this time.

"Are you still there?"

"Yes, sorry." Lotte cleared her throat. "I believe we have the same person in mind."

The conversation lasted awhile longer, but it mostly involved Lotte Jones talking and Priscilla listening. As the monologue continued, Lotte's coolness disappeared. She was almost eighty or, as she put it, about to celebrate "the big eight-oh." She had settled in the States after marrying a GI. They'd lived in Grand Forks, North Dakota ("a good place for a nice German girl to settle"), where her husband had "made a bundle in winter wheat." After he died, she moved to Coconut Beach, Florida.

"People call it God's waiting room, but I love it here."

She had no more questions and never mentioned Jake's name again. Instead, she went on and on about children, grandchildren, and how widows were all on the make for the few eligible men around the pool at her condo. She volunteered at a local hospital, she added, and played shuffleboard and cribbage with friends.

Finally, after another silence, she got around to what she really wanted to say.

"I'll be in Boston next week. I've already made the plane reservation. I know it's a bit awkward to ask since I'm a stranger to you, but I'd like to come out to Egg Rock for a short visit. Only for an hour or so. There are things I just can't tell you on the phone, and I have something to show you."

Priscilla sat for a long time after hanging up, wondering if she'd lost her mind. Maybe this woman was one of those con artists who preyed on the elderly. There were stories in the papers about them all the time.

But they had already made a date. When Priscilla suggested Lotte meet Jacob too, Lotte begged off, and they arranged for her to come later on the day he'd be leaving for home.

In spite of promising her friend Gretchen she'd tell Jacob everything, she'd been backsliding lately, hoping to put it off again, but this chatty widow from Florida, about whom she knew next to nothing, was going to make it impossible to keep stalling.

Glenda, the cleaning lady, would be there soon. She was no kid herself but could still make it up to the attic and locate the small suitcase.

Priscilla carried her cup to the parlor and sat under the watercolor Gretchen had painted for her fortieth birthday. By then, royalty checks were coming in regularly, so she could commission the work.

Priscilla Crane and Jessie Benton Fremont faced each other from opposite sides of the room.

It took a leap of faith to imagine that the young woman eyeing Priscilla from the frame was Priscilla too.

Her young version, done at a forty-five-degree angle, had jet-black hair cut short, with a part on the left side. A small widow's peak gave her a touch of the exotic, as did the hint of a cleft in her chin. Her eyebrows were meticulously trimmed, and her nose was slightly turned up. She was tanned, with no makeup except for shockingly red lipstick. If she could have a do-over, she'd tone down the lipstick, but that was it.

Glenda arrived, as always, at eight thirty on the dot. Priscilla was amazed how the woman did it. Her arrival time never deviated, but it wasn't as if she lived around the corner. Priscilla was convinced she left her house on the far side of Squimset at the crack of dawn and parked down the street so she could make a stage entrance.

*Stage entrance* was an appropriate term since Glenda, in her younger days, had sung with a popular local band. Priscilla had first met her years back, when she'd been involved with the Squimset shoe workers' strike, and she remembered holding baby Glenda in her arms on the picket line.

"Remember, it's a small overnight case tucked under an old awning—cream colored with brown trim."

Glenda nodded impatiently, as if she needed no reminders, and she set the bag in front of Priscilla minutes later.

A rotten-egg smell greeted Priscilla as soon as she unfastened the latches.

On top were three manila envelopes. The first contained the Kansas driver's license, the second held the oversize aviator glasses, and the third contained the leather bracelet. Underneath them sat a bundle of newspapers loosely held together with string—the obvious source of the smell. The paper was stained black here and there, but she could read an ad featuring men's suits at Jordan Marsh—"$29 with Extra Pair of Pants"—on an unstained section. Inside, the black rubberized wetsuit had shrunk to a hard mass the size of a baked potato.

Jacob and Katie arrived in the afternoon. Priscilla was dozing in her chair when the doorbell rang. She thought Glenda would let them in, until she remembered that Glenda was already gone for the day. Before she could make it to the door, they were inside.

*An unusual but attractive couple,* she thought. *Tall and short, light and dark—a perfect example of how opposites attract.*

They had met at a freshman mixer at Middlebury and been a couple ever since. Priscilla, in spite of her lifelong commitment to social justice, had been caught off guard—and upset in a way she never would have expected—when Jacob brought Katie home for the first time. Katie was actually Kaede; she'd been born in Kyoto but brought to the States as a newborn when her parents emigrated.

Jacob had been interested in languages for as long as she could remember, always pulling flashcards from his pocket and silently mouthing the words. By the time he'd gotten to Middlebury, he was proficient, if not fluent, in a half dozen languages. After meeting Kaede, he'd concentrated on the Far East, done graduate work in Japan and spent his entire career doing linguistic research at a small college in California.

Over supper, they talked about their plans for this time home—a game at Fenway and a day trip to the Cape—and Kaede got up to clear the table. It always fascinated Priscilla how couples worked together. Kaede, a decent linguist herself, preferred to be thought of as a wife and mother. Priscilla wondered whether her daughter-in-law's immersion in that role made it easier for the two of them to work as a unit.

Priscilla was hardly an expert on long-term domestic relationships, but she felt that couples in the same line of work didn't have things so easy. Gretchen and her artist husband, who'd ended up suing each other for assault and battery, were an extreme example.

At fifty-five—she had to rework the math in her head to be sure of his age—Jacob had faded blond rather than gray hair, and he kept it militarily short. His face was unlined and unblemished except for darkening under the eyes. His chin was a bit too long and tapered. If he'd been a politician, editorial cartoonists would have had a field day with it.

She had the crazy idea, and not for the first time, that this man sitting at her kitchen table and talking about being home wasn't her son at all. In the past, she'd tried to explain it away because he'd been away for so many years, lived at the other end of the country (which she'd never visited on account of her fear of flying), and had married into and devoted his life to something totally alien. The irony, of course, was that Jake Benz, the only man Priscilla had ever loved, had been no less of an alien himself.

No, Jacob looked like an imposter because she'd spent years fictionalizing him.

The questions began the day Jacob started kindergarten, but Priscilla had long been waiting for that day, and she was ready.

She told him she was actually not his mother but his aunt. Her brother, Henry, and his wife, Beatrice, Jacob's biological parents, had been killed in a car crash when he was a month old, and Priscilla had adopted him right away. There were no other family members.

What she didn't say was that her brother, Henry, her only sibling, had fallen through the ice and drowned, at age ten.

Jacob accepted Priscilla's explanation, as any five-year-old would have, but as he grew, he kept bringing up more questions. Priscilla constructed an elaborate backstory that expanded like the plot of one of her novels. She turned her drowned baby brother into a successful businessman with a paper mill and patterned her fictional sister-in-law, Beatrice, after her friend Gretchen.

The deception grew so complex that she took detailed notes to keep the narrative consistent and logical.

One Christmas, when Jacob was home from college, he confronted her, accusing her of withholding information that he was entitled to know. However, he spoke so timidly and apologetically that she decided to take the upper hand—by stonewalling.

It was a nasty scene. He raised his voice in a way she'd never heard before, she became tearful, and he marched out of the room.

The next morning, Jacob greeted his mother as if nothing had happened, but from then on, a new formality entered their relationship—and never went away.

The ninetieth birthday party was vintage Priscilla: a Sunday afternoon clambake on Curlew Beach, with Glenda and her son, Cecil, in charge. Dr. Leo Mulcahy and his wife, Claire, came up from Boston, and good old Gretchen went AWOL—her term—from an assisted-living facility to attend. Other than her longtime agent and Jacob and Kaede, all the other guests were Egg Rock friends. On Priscilla's orders, there were no speeches, gifts, singing, or cake, but champagne flowed freely.

Gretchen, her chair pushed around by an aide, was the life of the party, bubbling over with stories and an off-color joke or two. When she found a moment alone with Priscilla, however, she turned philosophic.

"I'm at the point in my life where I want to leave everything neat and clean with no loose ends."

"Don't worry. I'll tell Jacob everything before he leaves."

"No cold feet?"

"Nope, not this time."

The next day was the last of Jacob and Kaede's visit, and they made it their Boston day, with a harbor cruise, an afternoon ball game at Fenway, and early supper at a favorite Back Bay bistro. True to form, Priscilla waited until they got back to Egg Rock to have The Conversation.

The little brown-and-cream suitcase was sitting on the kitchen table when they came in.

"I need to speak to you about your father."

If Jacob was surprised, he didn't let on.

She began with the New Year's morning when Jake Benz washed up on the beach, and she told them all she remembered from the next two weeks, ending with the night he committed suicide and she buried the body. At appropriate moments, she handed them the remains of the rubber wetsuit, the oversize goggles, the Kansas driver's license, and the leather bracelet.

Jacob listened carefully, his unlined face expressionless.

When Kaede got up for a glass of water, he spoke for the first time.

"I found out about Uncle Henry when I was in college."

Priscilla's eyebrows went up.

"The library had the Boston papers on microfilm by then, so I scrolled through the pages, looking for clues. I did it once in a while, making a hobby of it. But one Saturday afternoon, after months of searching, there it was: a small paragraph tucked at the bottom of a back page. The headline was 'Ten-Year-Old Falls Thru Ice, Drowns.'"

98

"That Christmas when I wouldn't tell you—"

"That was just after I found the article."

For the first time in years, Jacob gently wrapped his hand around his mother's. "I suspected you weren't telling me the truth for a long time, but coming face-to-face with the evidence got me really spooked. I talked to Kaede about the evening you—"

"Stonewalled."

"And we agreed that you must have had a good reason to do what you did. So I decided to leave it at that and get on with my life. In a way, I was relieved because I was still afraid to find out who I really was."

He turned to Kaede, who nodded, and added, "But I'm not afraid anymore."

Once Priscilla was certain she was pregnant, she called Gretchen, who knew exactly what to do. The obstetrician she recommended was competent and discreet and had an arrangement with a private hospital tucked away in a rural area west of Boston.

Rockledge was a rambling Victorian that—except for a new wing with two delivery suites, a newborn nursery, and an up-to-date operating room—looked more like a posh resort than a hospital. The grounds were spacious, with tennis courts, a swimming pool, and hiking trails, while a guardhouse at the end of a winding driveway ensured total privacy.

Meanwhile, Gretchen agreed to housesit while Priscilla was "visiting family out of state."

Priscilla delivered a healthy eight-pound baby boy on October 7, 1945, and brought the baby home to Egg Rock in early November.

"What about my birth certificate?"

"Rockledge provided a lawyer who made rounds like one of the doctors. He was a white-haired man in a three-piece suit who always spoke as if he were addressing the court. He apparently had connections and could make things happen. On his first visit, he asked lots of questions about my family, and when I mentioned Henry's accident, he nodded his head gravely and wrote it down.'"

A few days after Priscilla had given birth, the lawyer returned with a briefcase full of documents to sign. Finally, he held up a sheet of parchment that looked like a diploma. "You must keep this in a safe place," he boomed.

"I was on top of the world. I had a beautiful baby named Jacob Henry Crane—and papers. Being legitimate isn't so important today, I guess, but back then, it meant everything."

At that, she sat back in her chair, drained. She'd told Leo about these moments of profound fatigue, when all she could do was be still and wait for the feeling to pass.

But she had one more thing on her mind: the phone call from Lotte Jones.

"She insisted on coming tomorrow after you leave."

By then, she'd gotten a second wind, and the three of them talked well into the night.

Jacob's reaction surprised her. Instead of getting angry or withdrawn, he grew more animated as they talked, reminding her of the boy she once had known so well.

Her only regret was having waited so long to tell the truth.

He had Priscilla repeat everything she'd told him earlier and urged her to describe his father in as much detail as she could recall.

"So I look a bit like him?"

"More than a bit, dear."

Before going upstairs, Jacob asked to take the wetsuit and other items back with him. A colleague who was an expert in forensic DNA analysis might have some luck, he explained.

Then he kissed his mother good night for the first time in years.

Priscilla awoke before dawn and had the coffeepot perking by the time Jacob and Kaede got downstairs.

With the cab due any minute, the luggage was stacked by the door. Jacob pointed to the cream-colored overnighter with brown trim.

"I'm keeping that little treasure chest safe and sound right under the seat."

Glenda arrived on schedule, turned on the little TV so she could watch her programs, and started tidying up the kitchen. Like most mornings, Priscilla sat at the table, nursing a second cup of coffee, while Glenda worked.

*They should be in the air,* she thought, already anticipating their next trip east at Christmas.

Glenda dropped the silverware she was rinsing into the sink with a clatter and turned up the volume.

Smoke was billowing out of the side of a skyscraper.

"Do you see that?"

But Priscilla was slumped forward, facedown, with coffee spreading across the table and dripping onto the floor.

Glenda was shaking so hard that she could barely dial 911.

Lotte Jones was about to have an adventure. She was so keyed up that she called the cab way earlier than necessary, checked her bag in no time, and was at the gate a whole hour before takeoff.

Instead of buying a magazine, she sat quietly, trying to focus on what a *komisch* turn her life had taken.

It had begun with a phone call out of the blue two weeks earlier. The woman had identified herself only as Gretchen, and Lotte figured she'd made the name up. As soon as Lotte identified herself, Gretchen started in.

Gretchen asked if Lotte recognized the name Jakob Benz, born in 1916 and missing in the war.

Lotte nearly dropped the phone.

Jakob was an American who taught school in her little town in Germany. He was a good-looking man, although a couple of centimeters shorter than she was and more than a couple of kilos lighter. The war had been going on for years by then, and things were getting hard, with more and more bombings. In fact, they were walking out of the town hall cellar after a raid when he asked her, "Would you like to get married?" Just like that. No flowers, no ring—just a simple question.

They got their marriage license upstairs in the same building the next day, and a week after that, he boarded a train with orders to report to someone somewhere. He couldn't say more. That was it—one week married.

After Jakob left, things got worse and worse. People started stripping bark off trees to boil for soup. Even the building where they were married was destroyed.

Later, during the occupation, she married another American, Jerry Jones. They moved to North Dakota, and as time passed, the one-week marriage to Jakob Benz blended into her other memories of the war. However, she still thought about him from time to time and wondered what had happened to him. He was too small to be a soldier, but by then, they were using old men and little boys to defend the fatherland.

The memories had ebbed, but the minute Gretchen called, they came flooding back.

Lotte looked up to see other passengers gathered around TVs, and the whole terminal, usually bustling, got as quiet as a church. Joining the others, she saw the print at the bottom of the screen: "World Trade Center Disaster."

Smoke was pouring out of an ugly black hole on the side of a skyscraper.

They all stood clustered around the monitors, watching the horror unfold. Meanwhile, no planes flew in or out. Nobody said a word until a big red-faced man in a Red Sox cap stumbled by the group, yelling, "We're next! We're next!"

Finally, there came an announcement that all flights were canceled and passengers could pick up their checked luggage downstairs at baggage claim.

In the cab, Lotte tried to concentrate on the oblivious palm trees lining the road back to the condo.

She decided to put off calling Priscilla since the phone lines would be tied up. They'd reschedule later.

The briefcase containing the only letter Jakob had ever sent, along with a handful of faded snapshots, sat on the seat beside her. Gretchen had suggested she bring them along.

On the phone, she'd asked Gretchen how she'd tracked down Lotte Jones, one of a zillion widows in the state of Florida.

"I guess there's no harm in telling you everything," she replied. "What are they going to do to a sweet little old lady like me anyway?"

Boston had a small but effective pro-German underground during the war. It had been a select group made up of academics, scientists, and government officials. They'd even been able to recruit a handful of police. One or two police chiefs from nearby towns had been exceptionally helpful. She'd been picked for her artistic skills, and in late 1944, she'd been ordered to prepare documents for a spy to be dropped offshore by U-boat.

"I was told his real name later on, and after the war, my husband learned that Jake's wife had married a GI named Jerry Jones and moved to North Dakota. The rest was easy to trace."

Lotte finally found the courage to ask the most important question of all. "What happened to Jakob?"

"I can't say, Lotte, but I'm sure Priscilla Crane will fill you in when you see her."

# $\mathscr{H}$OW BEAR POND GOT ITS NAME

The Egg Rock Vets' Club was jumping in the spring of 1946. Started by men returning from World War I, it had become a go-to party place in the twenties and a refuge for veterans down on their luck during the Depression, but this was something altogether different. Membership was at an all-time high with the return of  another war's veterans, and with so many not working yet, the club was in high gear day and night.

So it was no surprise when Joseph Steele Jr. found two bartenders already hard at work at four o'clock on a Monday afternoon. Joey slid into the only seat at the bar, right next to Vinnie Mulcahy, a kid he'd known since first grade. Vinnie had ended up in the Pacific—or, more accurately, over the Pacific—as a navigator in a B-29. He and Vinnie had been friendly rivals all their lives, going head-to-head in the classroom and on the ball fields. However, after coming home from the war, their lives diverged. Vinnie had his sights on law school, while Joey had no plans at all.

Since Joey was a regular, a Narragansett draft appeared under his nose automatically.

Vinnie had just launched into a story, and Joey asked him to start over. Vinnie had been telling stories for as long as Joey could remember, and he had mastered the art. Whenever anyone asked how he'd become so skilled, he'd credit his family. "I'm just repeating stuff I've been hearing since chowing down Pabulum in my high chair." Then, sounding like the lawyer he planned to be, he'd admit to adding a few flourishes of his own.

Vinnie's best ones took place in Egg Rock, and the best of the best were from a long time back. This sounded like one of Vinnie's history lessons, and Joey didn't want to miss a word.

Vinnie's stories about the old days had a way of settling him down. Joey still wasn't sleeping much, and the incessant nightmares made him jumpy and irritable. His father had commented on Joey's mood on Sunday. The old man never touched a drop all week, but at Sunday dinner, he'd throw back a couple of shots in rapid succession. So Sunday was the only day he'd string more than three words together.

"Junior, you've been hanging around the house since Thanksgiving. How many months does that make?" He held up his closed fist and unleashed one stubby finger, piston-like, at a time. "I'd think that after five months, you could get off your can. Your mother tells me you're in bed half the day and have your nose in a book the other half. Then, while the rest of us are trying to sleep, you're roamin' the house, doing God knows what. You've got a good head on your shoulders, Son. With all that reading, you could be teaching school, or with the engineering you learned in the service, I could get you a job on the line at the Westinghouse plant in Squimset tomorrow morning."

Joey had sat there with his head tilted, as if he were listening to a far-off voice. The old man had been about to continue, when Joey's mother had laid her hand on his arm.

Joe Senior was right, of course. He had to get his life on track, but he wasn't ready.

Vinnie broke off his story and cheerfully agreed to take it from the top. As far as Vinnie Mulcahy was concerned, the bigger the audience, the better.

"Picture what it must have been like in Egg Rock on a summer morning back in 1710. There were no streets, no houses, and no people. The land was covered with meadows and small patches of scrub since the trees that once covered the island had been chopped down for firewood.

"It must have been pretty quiet, since the only full-time inhabitants were sheep and cows. Egg Rock was grazing land for the people from the village of Squimset on the mainland. The only way to get out to Egg Rock by land was to wait for low tide and walk across the sandbar. Of course, we have a road today, but it didn't get built until much later.

"Before dawn, two brothers from Squimset hiked out to Egg Rock to hunt. There was no big game out here, just birds, rabbits, and, if they were lucky, a nice big turtle. Once there, the men split up. The first brother was surprised to encounter a seal sunning itself on the beach. Seals love to sunbathe but usually chose rocks offshore, where it's safer. He killed it, left the remains to carry back home later in the day, and went into the brush to see what else he could find. When he returned, he got another surprise: a full-grown black bear was feasting on the dead seal. The man broke into a run, but the bear easily outran him and clawed away most of his clothes before he finally escaped by jumping into a small pond nearby. The other man returned to find his brother still treading water and in no hurry to get out, even though the bear was long gone. On their way home, they kept their fowling pieces ready, but the bear didn't come back.

"Once the townsfolk heard the boys' story, they built a bonfire on the Squimset end of the sandbar to keep the bear from escaping during the night. The last thing they needed was a bear banqueting on their livestock. Squimset was pretty well settled by that time, and bears were infrequent visitors. No one could recall a bear making its way out to Egg Rock.

"Travelers between Squimset and Salem often encountered

bears in the dense woods between the two towns, so it was likely that the Egg Rock intruder had wandered out of the woods and gotten lost.

"At low tide the next morning, a search party left for Egg Rock, cornered the lost bear, and killed it.

"That's the sad story of how Bear Pond got its name."

The story done, Vinnie jumped off his stool, dropped some change onto the bar, and said good night. Everyone in Egg Rock knew that he was marrying Madeleine Coates the first week in June. Actually, Vinnie and his brother were both getting married—Vinnie to Madeleine and Walter to her identical twin, Patricia. The double ring ceremony would be a first for the town. Meanwhile, Vinnie was attending night school in Boston, so he had plenty to do.

Joey downed more beers, all the while trying to pull himself back to the 1700s, when life was much simpler. However, he couldn't get away from imagining how terrified those brothers would have been if they'd hiked out that morning to find themselves in the middle of the Egg Rock of 1946—except at Bear Pond.

The pond sat in the middle of an old golf course that had run out of money during the Depression. By the end of the war, the fairways were overgrown, the sand traps were unrecognizable, and the greens were obliterated. The pond, some fifty feet across and deep enough to hide decades of errant golf balls, had been a perfect water hazard. With the golf course forgotten, Bear Pond, unlike the rest of the world, had gone backward in time.

Since the vets' club overlooked the old golf course, Joey stepped outside on his way back from the head to have a look, but it was hidden in the darkness.

He stuck around until closing. Others came and sat at the bar, but barely anyone spoke to him. Since coming home, he'd become argumentative, especially after a few beers, so most guys gave him a wide berth.

On the way home, he made a detour to the pond. In the moonlight, he hoped it would look the way it had in Vinnie's story.

He wasn't disappointed.

At that hour, the houses on the far side of the abandoned course were dark. The waning moon barely allowed him to navigate the path, but it had transformed the pond into a big silver disk that reminded Joey of a giant, highly polished fifty-cent piece.

He pulled off his shoes, rolled up his trousers, and lowered his feet into the water. The coldness was a shock at first, reminding him that the pond was spring-fed and frigid, keeping the pond iced in for hockey late in the season. Even in late August, when Egg Rock had its best beach days, Bear Pond remained unswimmable.

In no time, his feet numbed up, so he stayed put.

He hadn't felt such cold water since the bridge. *That goddamned bridge!* The bridge was front and center in his brain just about all the time, but the whole evening had gone by without his going there. The beers helped some, but it was Vinnie's story that had let him switch gears and concentrate on the hunters, the seal, the sandbar, the bear, the bonfire, and the pond, and push the bridge aside for a few hours.

Just then, with his feet still dangling in the water, he got a crazy idea. What if he made the bridge into a story? He knew the facts by heart, but up till then, he'd had no one to share it with. If he told it like a story, maybe he could tame it and file it away like one of Vinnie's stories.

Since coming home, he'd been bingeing on war stories. Miss Pettigrew at the library had helped him compile a reading list. *All Quiet on the Western Front* was his odds-on favorite. *The Red Badge of Courage*, which he'd never appreciated in high school; *For Whom the Bell Tolls*; and *Paths of Glory* had made the list. Last but not least, Miss Pettigrew had included *The Iliad*—to drive home the message that the horrors of war were as old as civilization itself.

After moving his legs around to make sure they were still attached, Joey began reciting his own story out loud, pretending Vinnie was sitting right there beside him.

"Our squad of engineers had been given a straightforward assignment the morning after the Germans retreated: keep the bridge in one piece. It was the first opening across the Rhine for Allied troops and, in Eisenhower's words, 'worth its weight in gold.' The Germans had tried to blow it up before they retreated, but the bridge had other ideas.

"We weren't engineers in the strictest sense, only guys who'd been picked for the job because we were good with our hands. Like me, the other guys had put together crystal sets, built tree houses in their backyards, and worked on their old man's Model A. We all loved to tinker with things—but not with half the world shooting at us.

"When the men complained about the icy water, the first sergeant was always ready.

"'Alpine runoff,' he'd answer, gesturing south with a cigarette jammed between his yellowed teeth, sounding like the geologist he had been before the war.

"One of the guys loved to sing, and one of his favorites was the nursery rhyme 'London Bridge Is Falling Down.' His name was Edmund Spenser—same as some long-ago English poet, he said—and since he'd been a high school teacher before the war, everyone believed him. He knew every verse, and by the time we'd been on the bridge a couple of days, we all did.

"Listening to 'London Bridge' was a lot like listening to one of Vinnie Mulcahy's stories. It carried me back to a simpler time and made me feel like a kid again.

"Once he started singing, he'd go through all twelve verses. Sometimes the rest of us would join in, but whether it was a solo or group effort, it became a daily routine. One night over supper, someone asked what the nursery rhyme was all about, and Eddie Spenser the engineer became a history teacher once again. The verses of the rhyme, he explained, traced the history of the bridge from its earliest days, when it was made of wood and clay, to stone, brick, and, finally, steel. He described the different bridges in detail, with their arches, towers, walkways, and shops. He even told us about an early battle in which the Vikings brought the bridge down.

"'Some things never change!' muttered one guy.

"Since our bridge was carrying troops and vehicles across the Rhine day and night, the Germans aimed their artillery, floated their mines, and even managed to get a few tactical bombers in the air, all with one objective: to put this shortcut to the heart of the fatherland—and a quick end to the war—out of commission.

"It felt like all the firepower of the Third Reich was zeroing in on us, but we just kept patching up the old bridge and singing:

Iron and steel will bend and bow,
bend and bow, bend and bow.
Iron and steel will bend and bow,
my fair lady.

"The simple rhyme was like the abracadabra of a magician or

the incantations of a priest. It made us feel invincible. Near misses damaged the bridge time after time, but without a direct hit, it survived—and so did we. Until late on the tenth day.

"In the morning, we heard an odd, high-pitched whine, which the first sergeant recognized immediately.

"'Jesus Christ! V-2s!' he yelled.

"The rockets missed too but not by much. We watched nearby barracks blow apart and collapse into burning piles of debris. With each hit, the bridge shook like it never had before, and all we could do was look at each other. Eddie Spenser, silent for once, simply shrugged.

"The bridge held together, so we kept fortifying the roadway while trucks, tanks, and troops kept rolling above us. I was some twenty feet outside of the west tower with Eddie Spenser just below me, when it happened.

"Before I heard a thing, the soles of my feet began to tingle. I figured they'd gone to sleep from being in the same position too long, so I stamped. There was no reason to be worried at that point since there had been no artillery fire, no mortars, no airstrike, and no floating mines. Not even any wind.

"But the tingling soon became a generalized vibration, and a humming sound kicked in, as if something deep inside the structure had gone haywire. As the hum reached a crescendo, the entire assembly suddenly shifted to one side, listed like a sinking ship, and began coming apart. Metal chunks showered down all around us and splashed into the fast-moving river below. Eddie was methodically tightening bolts, and when the structure shifted, the beam he was standing on broke free. He grasped one of the crossbars with both hands while his feet swung free below with nothing to land on. By the time he looked up, I was already scrambling down to pull him back. He fixed his eyes on me, but just as I got to him, he shook his head, let go, hit the water, and disappeared. I made it back to the tower the instant the entire center span gave way.

"We lost twenty-eight engineers, including Eddie Spenser, that afternoon."

The story done, Joey slid into the pond. The water stung like hell until, like his legs, his whole body numbed up.

He started singing, using every ounce of lung power to make it sound as if a whole chorus of engineers were belting out the tune.

He reached the end of the third verse:
Wood and clay will wash away,
wash away, wash away.
Wood and clay will wash away,
my fair lady.

Suddenly, he heard someone running. He pictured a hunter trying to outrun a bear.

"Joey, grab this, and I'll pull you to shore!"

He followed orders since he was so paralyzed by the cold that he'd never make it out of the pond on his own.

Vinnie Mulcahy helped Joey into his shoes and threw his jacket over his shoulders.

"I was heading home from Madeleine's, when I decided to check out the pond. Funny, I never come this way. From the road, I could see how stunning it is in the moonlight. I stood admiring the view, when somebody started singing at the top of his lungs. That's when I started running. I found this hockey stick lying on the ground. No wonder some kid left it behind, with this big crack in it."

Vinnie never asked him the obvious question: What the Christ was Joey Steele doing treading water in Bear Pond in the middle of the night, singing a stupid nursery rhyme loudly enough to wake the dead?

Since Joey had no coherent explanation, he didn't try to invent one.

They were halfway to Joey's house when he finally spoke.

"I liked the Bear Pond story, Vinnie. A lot. But it got me thinking."

"I know. Stories get you thinking, and you never know where they'll take you."

"I need to tell you another story. I know it's late, but it's important."

Joey ran upstairs to change while Vinnie waited in the Steeles' kitchen. Then, over warmed-up coffee from his mom's pot, he told Vinnie about how he couldn't save Eddie Spenser from a falling bridge. Since he'd already given the story a trial run at Bear Pond, it went off smoothly.

Vinnie lit a cigarette. He looked as cool as ever, but his hands were shaking. "Thanks, Joey."

"I should be the one with the thank-yous! If you hadn't shown up, I'd be at the bottom of the pond with all those golf balls."

"I mean it, Joey. I'm not brave enough to tell a story like that." He took another drag before continuing. "Does it help to put it into words?"

"You know, Vinnie, I'm only sure about one thing right now."

"What's that?"

"I'm gonna sleep like a baby tonight."

# $\mathcal{M}$ARY, MARY

Mary Frances Tierney was a pretty girl. In fact, everybody agreed she was the prettiest girl in Egg Rock. Okay, not every single person in the town agreed, but it must have been around 99 percent.

The best part was that she hadn't let that fact go to her head.

Age-wise, she was smack in the middle of a fair-sized family. Of course, that was 1948, when families double the size of the Tierney clan were a dime a dozen. Junior (Thomas Jr.) and Mary Celeste were the oldest; Mary Frances was the third in line; Richie was behind her by two years; and their mom had, as Aunt Ellie liked to put it, another one in the oven.

It would have been no surprise for such a family to be growing, unless one knew the kids' ages. You see, Richie, at present the youngest, was about to turn eighteen.

Everyone knew that Kate Tierney was going to have a change-of-life baby—another of Aunt Ellie's phrases. When Mary Frances first heard the term, she had some questions for Mary Celeste, who, at twenty-two, was the most worldly-wise girl she could confide in— and her only source of information in the pregnancy department.

But she wished she hadn't asked. You see, Mary Celeste was attending nursing school in Boston, and she had already rotated on the labor and delivery floor at Saint Katherine's Hospital. She loved to tell real-life stories that made Mary Frances feel a little sick to her stomach. Besides, she was sure her older sister made a lot of stuff up as she went along, the way she had when they were younger.

"Near menopause, a woman's periods get irregular, and her hormones"—it was the first time Mary Frances had heard the word, but again, it was 1948—"get so intense that she can get pregnant just by touching a man's underwear."

Mary Frances remembered finding a caterpillar on the screened-in porch when she was just a little girl. Mary Celeste came along and, with the self-assurance of a biology professor, launched into a lecture about the caterpillar's life cycle. The only problem was, as Mary Frances learned later in a real biology class, caterpillars eventually turned into butterflies instead of the other way around.

The Tierney-Rhinehart clan had two events to celebrate—Aunt Ellie's birthday and Mary Frances's graduation—so Kate Tierney invited both sides of the family for Sunday dinner.

Aunt Ellie showed up early to give a hand, but Kate insisted that she sit in the kitchen while Mary Celeste and Mary Frances helped out. Meanwhile, Tommy and Richie were dispatched to the attic to lug down the two heavy oak leaves for the dining room table.

Aunt Ellie was the most independent woman Mary Frances had ever met. The day after Pearl Harbor, she was gung-ho to enlist, but old Mr. Rhinehart, a veteran who'd seen "plenty," as he put it at the time, begged his daughter not to. So she did the next best thing by taking leave from her job at the bank, joining the Red Cross, and shipping off to England. Mary Frances's mother made vague reference to her getting engaged to an RAF pilot who went missing in action, but Aunt Ellie never said a word about it.

When Mary Frances was younger, she spent many an overnight at Aunt Ellie's apartment in Squimset and would accompany her to Squimset Savings, drawing pictures while Aunt Ellie worked at her desk. She'd go to lunch in downtown Squimset with Ellie and other women from the bank.

By the time Mary Frances was in high school, Aunt Ellie would invite her out to dinner once in a while. That usually meant eating in a nice restaurant since Aunt Ellie would be the first to tell anybody that she "couldn't boil water."

At one of those dinners, she met a newly hired teller. Freddie Jean Myles had worked as a stewardess for Pan American Airways until she reached the mandatory retirement age of thirty-two. The woman was so poised and professional looking, Mary Frances thought. When she talked about flying to places like Chicago, San Francisco, and even Honolulu, Mary Frances wondered how this woman had gotten so lucky. With senior year looming, she had no real plans for the future. Nursing school, normal school, and secretarial school were really the only options, and none of those interested her at all. When her father offered to see about an opening in the office at the plant, she had a frightful vision of getting on the bus to Squimset every morning for the rest of her life. She knew she'd rather die.

In the days following the dinner, Mary Frances found herself daydreaming about the attractive, worldly woman who knew her way around the Golden Gate, Waikiki, night clubs, and luxury hotels. One night, she dreamed she was a full-fledged stewardess herself, regal in a perfectly fitted blue suit and matching hat, serving Gregory Peck a martini in the first-class cabin.

Aunt Ellie, always a step ahead of everybody else, arranged another get-together with Freddie Jean Myles without Mary Frances ever asking.

"They don't just take any kid out of high school," the retired stewardess said. The fact that she'd been to nursing school made the difference in her own case, she added, since she was better equipped to deal with the inevitable blocked ears and air sickness as well as a serious medical emergency.

"Your aunt tells me you're a pretty good French student," she continued. "Build on that, and they might consider you for international flights." She handed Mary Frances a big manila envelope with the Pan Am trademark on the front. "Homework," Freddie Jean Myles added with a smile.

The summer following high school graduation, Mary Frances landed the ideal job. A customer at Aunt Ellie's bank needed a live-in assistant for her elderly mother, who'd recently arrived from France. By the time Mary Frances applied for a stewardess position a year later, she was reading French novels and thinking in French half the time.

It was the longest questionnaire she'd ever seen, asking everything from vital statistics, such as her birth date, height, weight, and eye and hair color, to education, work history, hobbies, and a million other things.

The essay section, which was to be no more than three hundred words and double-spaced, with one carbon copy, took the most time to write, and once she'd completed a first draft, she asked Aunt Ellie to look it over.

To fill out the two required character references, she chose Miss Pettigrew, the town librarian, and Clara, her boss at the market where she'd stocked shelves after school.

Freddie Jean took the afternoon off from the bank the day of Mary Frances's interview at a Boston hotel and went along to give her young friend moral support.

They had apparently read her application carefully, since her interviewer, an elegant older woman in a finely tailored suit, conducted the meeting entirely in French.

Uncle Dennis seemed pleased when Mary Frances came by for the required studio portraits. While setting up the big camera and getting the lights at just the right angle, he told her again and again how proud he was of her. But he sounded a little sad when he added, "Too many of us get trapped on this little island for life!"

The day the acceptance letter arrived was the happiest day of her life. Aunt Ellie hosted a celebratory dinner at the same restaurant where Mary Frances had first met Freddie Jean, and before she knew it, she was boarding a train to Miami.

Now she was home again, with her diploma and her wings. Her first assignment, only a week away, was as the newest hire on Pan Am's most prestigious route: New York to Paris.

Mary Frances knew it was only a matter of time before Aunt Ellie would get up from the Tierney's kitchen table and pitch in.

"So what if it's my birthday? I still have a right to peel the potatoes, don't I?"

Mary Frances's mother didn't object.

"Now, that's better. How are you feeling, Kate? I have to say, you look tired."

"I'm fine. I was at the doctor's Friday, and everything seems to be in order. But I can't wait for the baby to come. Only three weeks to go."

"What about names?"

"Tom and I have talked a little, but he's convinced it's going to be a boy, and he insists on naming him"—she bit her lip as if she'd cry any second—"Harry. He says that having the three boys called Tom, Dick, and Harry would be nifty.'"

"I say it's absurd."

All Kate could do was nod.

"What about girls' names, in case Tom's predictive powers fail him for once?"

"Well, you know how Father Winters feels."

"I really don't care what Father Winters feels about anything, let alone what the name of my newest niece or nephew's going to be."

"Please, Ellie, let's not start that. Not today."

Mary Frances had not been consulted, of course, but she could see that her mother was getting all sorts of advice and had no say in the matter.

The table was set, the roast was out of the oven, and the boys had rounded up the requisite chairs before the guests arrived.

Mary Frances's father carved, and the kids served. Kate raised her glass to toast her sister, remarking that Ellie Rhinehart was "keeping those bankers in Squimset honest for a change."

Once the laughter died down, Tom surveyed the room and raised his glass to Mary Frances, predicting that she was the kind of girl who'd be flying high in her new job, and as for his daughter's future, the sky was the limit.

His speech was met by the expected hisses and clapping.

The only worrisome thing was that Kate ate next to nothing and abruptly left the room a couple of times.

Over dessert, she excused herself a third time, and Mary Celeste followed close behind her mother.

They were no sooner out of the room than Aunt Ellie changed

the subject. It was a shame that Father Supple, the new curate at Saint Lawrence's, had needed to cancel at the last minute. With a priest at the table, Aunt Ellie could have asked her questions without risking a shouting match.

"So, Tom, you're predicting a boy?"

"No doubt in my mind."

It was not the first time Mary Frances had heard her father make such pronouncements. Every March, the foremen at the Westinghouse plant expected the employees to pick their two vacation weeks. Most chose the same weeks every year, but Tom Tierney claimed to have a secret, foolproof system to guarantee the two weeks between the Fourth of July and Labor Day with the best possible weather. Afterward, he'd always claim he'd "won again," but according to Tom Junior, they'd come out just about average each year. Junior was a bookkeeper at the plant and knew his way around numbers—as if Mary Frances needed further convincing.

Ellie persisted. "Any names in mind?"

"Only one. Harry."

"Tom, Dick, and Harry? Are you raising a family or forming a vaudeville act?"

Mary Frances glanced at the empty wine bottles on her mother's sideboard and sensed big trouble ahead.

The secret to the Tierney-Rhinehart family harmony was simple: steer clear of religion and politics. The Rhineharts were Protestants— Presbyterians to be exact—and Kate Rhinehart had converted to the Catholic church when she married Tom Tierney. Not only that, but the Rhineharts were Republicans to their last breath, and the Tierneys were dyed-in-the-wool Democrats.

Aunt Ellie got the ball rolling. "What if it's a girl? Will it be another Mary something? According to my sister, Father Winters expects every female on the face of the earth to be named Mary this or Mary that."

They had crossed the Rubicon. Once religion was in the mix, politics was sure to follow. With the election only weeks away, and with Dewey and Truman neck and neck, that meant fireworks.

The next minute, her father pointed at one of her Rhinehart cousins, calling him a son of a bitch.

Mary Frances closed her eyes and mentally transported herself to twenty thousand feet, floating above cotton-candy clouds on a sunny morning.

Things continued to go downhill, with everybody shouting, a glass or two smashing, and a chair tipping over—until Mary Celeste ran into the room in a panic.

"Get the doctor!"

Junior found Doc Kendrick at the new golf links, trying to chip out of a sand trap on the fourth hole. *New* wasn't quite the right word since the links had closed during the Depression and just reopened that spring.

Minutes later, the doctor rushed into the front hall and flew upstairs with his black bag tucked under his arm.

Meanwhile, Richie was dispatched to the rectory to summon a priest.

The waiting was the worst part. They all kept vigil in the dining room. Father Supple, the young curate just out of seminary, came right away and sat quietly like the others. Mary Frances was grateful it wasn't Father Winters, because he would have started reciting the rosary as soon as he got in the door, expecting the whole family to join in.

Fortunately, Kate Tierney had put the big coffeepot on the stove before excusing herself. Mary Frances started pouring and got Richie to deliver the steaming cups to the table. No one spoke. Her father looked serene, as if he already knew how things would turn out. Aunt Ellie sat ramrod straight in her chair, her eyes wide and, from what Mary Frances could see, never blinking. Father Supple, who looked more like a kid home from college than a priest, sat slightly hunched forward with his eyes closed.

She lost track of time. There was usually no problem keeping time in the Tierney house, with the big grandfather clock in the vestibule chiming dutifully every quarter hour. However, the only sound Mary Frances could hear was her mother's shrieks every few minutes.

Suddenly, there was a different sound: the unmistakable lusty cry of a newborn baby. Tom Tierney jumped out of his chair and, with his usual self-assurance, announced, "Atta boy, Harry!"

By then, everyone was on their feet, hugging and back-slapping. Tom Tierney left the room for a moment and returned with a box of Havana cigars.

One never could have imagined that they had been at each other's throats barely an hour earlier. Even her father's pronouncement about who had given that lusty cry upstairs went unchallenged.

They expected the doctor, or at least Mary Celeste, to come downstairs at any time with news, but the minutes dragged on. Finally, Father Supple started reciting the Our Father, and everybody, even Aunt Ellie, joined in.

Just then, Kate Rhinehart gave out another wail, louder than ever, and immediately, the baby began crying again—not as lustily this time but strongly enough. While everyone listened, Mary Celeste burst into the room again and frantically motioned to her father, Aunt Ellie, and the priest. All four hustled back upstairs, but within a couple of minutes, Ellie reappeared and stood in the doorway, looking cool and businesslike, as if she were about to address her fellow officers at the bank.

"Everybody is fine. Kate is thrilled but exhausted, of course. When I got upstairs, she was lying back comfortably with a smile like I haven't seen in years. She asked me to give you the news."

Everybody started talking at once until she raised her hands in mock horror. "Just let me finish! We have two new members of the clan—a girl and a boy!"

After another round of hugs, back-slapping, and glasses getting refilled, she broke in again. "There's more, if you care to hear. Kate has already chosen the names, and I imagine the young priest is baptizing them right now."

The room went silent.

"The firstborn is Eleanor, named, I'm told, for her stunning looks and authoritative voice. Looks like Tom struck out again."

She motioned for a glass of water and took a long pull. "Oh yes, the second baby. He arrived ten minutes after his sister but looks just as pink and healthy."

She waited a moment more for effect. "His name is Dewey Truman Tierney."

With that, she passed Tom's box of Havana cigars around the room and, with a flourish, lit one for herself.

# $\mathcal{T}$HE BLACK MINE

Walter Mulcahy was one of the first people I met after renting a small apartment in Egg Rock. I had just been discharged from the army and felt that working my way back into civilian life would be easier in such a quiet, out-of-the-way place.

I bumped into him on the rocky shore on the north side of town on the first real spring day after the brutal winter of 1954. Walking along the shore path near John's Peril, I caught sight of a gangly redheaded man in a checked shirt crouched at the shoreline, showing something to a little boy standing beside him.

The man waved and motioned me to join them.

"I was just showing Leo how crabs hide under rocks in the tide pools," he said without further introduction.

I thought he must have been mixing me up with someone he knew, but I soon learned that he always greeted strangers like old friends.

"I bet you didn't know that this was once called the Black Mine," he continued, pointing to an unimpressive jagged cliff nearby. "Although the work here ended three hundred years ago, the rocks haven't smoothed out yet. Erosion can take a very long time."

Sensing I was interested in hearing more, he motioned to a nearby boulder that was just the right height for me to sit on.

Once I was settled, he had Leo pick up a flat stone about the size of a half piece of toast, only heavier, and the boy dropped it into my hand. It was black, with some dark green mixed in, and covered with whitish speckles.

"You're holding a piece of gabbro. A few miles west of here, in Saugus, they're doing an archeologic dig at an iron works from colonial days, in the 1600s. Without the gabbro they found here, the iron works would never have gotten off the ground."

Gabbro, he explained, wasn't all that common. Seismic events millions of years back had pushed it to the surface from deep inside the earth. When mixed with the bog ore from Saugus and heated, the gabbro acted as a fluxing agent, extracting impurities from the ore and leaving pure iron. In England, limestone was used for flux, but gabbro did a much more efficient job. Egg Rock had the only deposit of gabbro close enough to be transported to the iron works.

That involved sailing down the Saugus River out into Squimset Bay, rounding the southern and eastern shores of Egg Rock, and landing at the Black Mine. Each trip took a full day or even more if the weather turned.

"From what I've read," he said, "something terrible happened at the Black Mine. Soon afterward, the iron works shut down for good."

I couldn't be sure how much of what he was saying was history and how much was just a tall tale, but I was so hooked by then that I didn't care.

Walter smiled and continued his story.

The mining crew of some dozen men stayed at Egg Rock, while the boat's crew, with a half dozen more men, made runs back and forth from Saugus. During the summer of 1661, the boat failed to come back as scheduled, and after a week of waiting, a second boat set out with a search party on board.

The iron works was owned and operated by an English company, but about half of its workers were Scottish prisoners of war. The arrangement seemed to work well, with no historical record of unrest or conflict with the prisoners, but the likelihood of mutiny must have crossed the minds of the search party.

The mining camp was deserted when the search party arrived. The boat used to transport the gabbro, called the *Makreel*, was missing, but nothing else was out of place. The mining tools sat on the ground, as if the workers had simply taken a break, and the living quarters were in order. Wherever they might have gone, they couldn't have taken much with them. Food, water, pots and pans, and clothing had been left behind, as if the men had expected to return the same day.

Piles of gabbro were neatly stacked at the shoreline, ready to be loaded for the next trip back to Saugus.

There was no sign of a struggle or bloodshed, making mutiny or an Indian attack unlikely.

The search party scoured Egg Rock for clues. The island's interior, mostly pasture, yielded nothing. They searched every inch of the shore, with its dozens of inlets and beaches, and found nothing there either. On the last day, they sailed along the island's perimeter, over the underwater ledges off what later became Forty Steps, and around Egg Rock itself, a half mile offshore. Still, they had no luck.

Finally, they collected as many of the miners' personal items as they could fit on their boat and left for Saugus.

It took a while for them to discover Amos Tower's diary. Mr. Tower was the leader of the mining crew and the only one allowed to bring more than a small satchel with him to Egg Rock. The diary was wrapped inside a spare set of pants, under his Bible, a bottle of rum, a half dozen clay pipes, and a pouch of tobacco, at the bottom of his trunk.

Saugus's only schoolteacher, the most learned man around and one of the few who could read and write, was given the job of examining the diary.

Exactly one page was given over to each day, and the entries were written in a tight, cramped script that filled every available space on the paper. Paper was shipped from England, so every sheet was precious. Mr. Tower chronicled the daily routine at the camp, the comings and goings of the *Makreel*, provisions consumed, and fish caught. On slow days, he turned his attention to the world around him. In one passage, he described a gaggle of gulls wheeling and pirouetting against a "shocking blue sky" on a bright, windy day, and in another, he wrote that the rays of the setting sun illuminated autumn leaves with a "rare vividness."

From time to time, however, his tone turned ominous. He described one sunrise as "a furnace into which we sinners will surely tumble."

The last entry in Amos Tower's diary, written some two weeks before the search party arrived, was filled with the usual observations, but on that date, Sunday, July 21, 1661, there was a second page.

As always, every inch of the page was filled, only this time with a magnificent drawing.

The sun sat at the horizon, illuminating a calm sea and a small sailing ship precariously tilted toward its bow, about to sink. Beneath the water's surface swam schools of fish, and in the distance, a whale spouted water toward the sky, where a pair of angels looked down on the scene.

That chance meeting at the Black Mine led to my decades-long friendship with Walter Mulcahy. Walter and his brother, Vincent, were already well-known lawyers by then, but they both loved the outdoors more than anything else. As Walter put it once, Vincent was the would-be meteorologist and astronomer, leaving Walter with "rocks, crabs, and jellyfish."

In a way, Walter and Patty adopted me. Patty often accompanied us on our hikes around the island, and their son, Leo, joined us until he got old enough to have friends of his own. Since I was a bachelor, Patty insisted I join the family for Sunday supper just to make sure I didn't starve.

All of that lasted until Walter and Patty were killed in a plane crash. Their plane was brought down by a terrorist bomb, about the first such incident in modern times. Of course, with 9/11 and all the other craziness in the world today, that shocking tragedy seems quaint by comparison.

It was 9/11, in fact, that got me thinking about Walter, Patty, and Leo, who, in spite of losing his family like that, became one of Boston's most respected doctors. It also got me thinking about the story of the Black Mine that Walter had told me many years before.

Life has been kind to me since those early days after my war. I opened a small restaurant in Squimset soon after meeting Walter and ended up with three busy Lobstah Maniah locations before selling out to a national chain for a small fortune.

But I still awaken in the middle of the night, going back over the terrible mistake I made as a newly promoted staff sergeant in Korea. The board of inquiry concluded that the friendly fire was a miscalculation, and I was spared the ordeal of a court-martial, but screwing up the trajectory and dropping a mortar shell on my own men is something I will never forgive myself for.

I'm retired now, but I still make it out to our VA hospital a couple of times a week. I was an auto mechanic way back when, and I still love to tinker. The opportunity to repair wheelchairs in the hospital's shop has turned out to be a perfect fit for me. I appreciate the anonymity of my work. The vets regain a bit of independence, and I stay in the background.

It must sound odd to you, but 9/11 made me think of a way to honor my friend Walter Mulcahy and maybe make amends for my battlefield mistake: solve the mystery of the Black Mine.

I had no doubt Walter would get a kick out of my getting to the bottom of his mystery, and I imagined the miners and sailors who'd disappeared so long ago would too. The older I get, the more connections I see. The men hit by friendly fire outside Pusan in the 1950s and the missing men of the Black Mine from the 1660s were born three hundred years apart and nearly half a world apart, but they are all brothers.

First, I wondered how much of Walter's story could be verified. He tended to get carried away and let his imagination take over.

I began by contacting Dr. Leo Mulcahy. The last time I'd seen him was at his parents' memorial service, when he was still a college student, but when I reintroduced myself on the phone, he remembered who I was.

He recalled the story of the missing miners too, calling it one of his father's favorite tales. He sounded enthusiastic about my plan and suggested coming out to Egg Rock in order to refresh his memory of the place.

We met on a sunny April afternoon, much like the day I'd first met Leo and his dad.

It was good omen, I thought.

However, a large fog bank sat offshore, not unusual for a spring day in Egg Rock.

Leo looked a lot like his mother; his dark hair was now flecked with gray, and he'd inherited her melt-your-heart smile. Patty Mulcahy had smiled just like that the night before she and Walter left for their vacation to Greece. Her biggest worry had been not flying halfway round the world but Leo, who was applying to medical school.

"How many classics majors make the cut?" she'd asked.

Leo was accompanied by a woman who looked about his own age, with similar salt-and-pepper hair. She had freckles on her nose and over her high cheekbones and wore steel-rimmed granny glasses.

"This is my cousin Portia, the town librarian," Leo said after shaking hands.

I had never set foot in the Egg Rock Public Library, but I remembered seeing her around town.

"She's interested in the Black Mine story too."

The three of us walked down to the abandoned mine site, and the first thing I found was a hunk of gabbro for them to examine.

Portia turned the small, speckled rock over in her hands, exposing wrists crisscrossed with horizontal scars. She looked up, met my eyes for a moment, and handed the rock to her cousin.

We poked around the remains of the mine and worked our way over rocks to the high ground, where there was a fine view of Little Egg Rock on the far side of Short Beach. It was hard to imagine how such an innocent-looking place could harbor any dark secrets.

Leo led us to the foot-path toward Forty Steps, where we walked along the water where the *Makreel* must have made its regular trips to and from the iron works. However, an east wind soon picked up, the sky grayed out, and the temperature plummeted.

Portia shrugged and led the way back as the visibility dropped to only a few feet. We proceeded over the rocky path single file, so close we could have been tethered together.

Once we made it back to the mine, she blew into her hands. "Time to get inside!"

I had been in the kitchen of her family's house once before, when her father, Vincent, was still alive. He'd invited me over to take a look at his little weather station one winter afternoon, and we'd ended up warming ourselves afterward by the same stove.

Over mugs of brandy-laced tea, I retold Walter Mulcahy's Black Mine story in as much detail as I could summon. Portia took pages of notes as I went along, raising her hand and asking me to repeat a detail here and there.

When I finished, she put down her pencil and took a deep breath. "Sounds like a tall tale, but I'll look into it."

A week later, Portia left a short message on my machine.

"Uncle Walter did his homework," she announced, and she invited me to the library to see for myself.

The Egg Rock Public Library is a jewel box of a building next door to the town hall. I guess you'd call it neo-Gothic style-wise, with its high-pitched slate roof and leaded windows.

We sat in Portia's cubbyhole of an office while she scrolled through the historical record of the Saugus Iron Works. In places, the details were amazing, with lists of employees, invoices, and transcripts of disciplinary hearings. One ledger of accounts noted that the *Makreel* had failed to return to Saugus from the mine in mid-July 1661, and a search party had been sent out in the beginning of August.

Amos Tower's diary, which Portia called our Holy Grail, was apparently lost, but excerpts from the diary popped up in a history of Squimset written in the nineteenth century. The passages that described the gulls cavorting in the wind under a "shocking blue sky" and the sunrise like hell's furnace were there. Portia had highlighted them in yellow marker so I wouldn't miss them.

Then she handed me a single sheet of paper. "I found this passage in a book called *The Wonders of the Invisible World*: *Observations as well*

*Historical as Logical upon the Nature, the Number, and the Operations of the Devils,* by Cotton Mather. I took the liberty of updating the language a bit."

> The story of a gentleman by the name of Tawyer illustrates the power of Satan, especially when the Devil appears, not as an evil and depraved human being, but as an honest and righteous man. Mister Tawyer, a natural leader, was able to use the Devil's wiles to seduce his men into believing that they were all so depraved and so sinful that they took their boat out to sea, sank it, and drowned.

I read the passage slowly three or four times just to make sure I was taking everything in. When I finally looked up, Portia was quietly stacking the books and papers she'd consulted into neat piles on her desk.

"Obviously, it's a stretch. The Reverend Mather makes no further mention of the incident, and I can't find any other mention of a 'Mister Tawyer' in what I've read."

"So what's the next step?"

"I'll continue to nose around, but I doubt anything else will turn up. Anyway, I can't imagine that there'd be much left of a three-hundred-year-old shipwreck, even if (a) 'Mister Tawyer' is our man and (b) if we had the faintest idea of where the *Makreel* might have gone down. I'm afraid we've reached a dead end."

Instead of going home, I walked up to Forty Steps, a great place to let your mind wander. On the clearest days, you can trace the coast all the way out to Gloucester.

It was hazy, but there was no fog bank to worry about. Egg Rock, barely a half mile offshore, shimmered in the late afternoon sun. The dead low tide exposed more of the rock's surface than usual, making it look even closer. Farther out, a couple of freighters were making their way south, when a lone sailboat came into view close to shore, probably heading back to the town wharf before nightfall. It was taking roughly the same route the *Makreel* must have sailed on its runs between the Black Mine and the Saugus Iron Works.

It was a handsome thirty-foot sloop, its mainsail taut in the breeze. Approaching Forty Steps, it suddenly tacked to the port, making me wonder if the crew realized they were nearly on top of Saunder's Ledge. Countless ships have wrecked on that ledge over the centuries, especially at low tide, when its jagged surface lies only a couple of feet under the water's surface. In fact, a lighthouse was erected on Egg Rock in part to warn ships away from the ledge.

It took several months for me to get my plan up and running.

Snow came early that fall, but it was followed by days of perfectly flat sea—what Portia called "the calm after the storm." By then, the team I'd hired had already mapped the area between Forty Steps and Egg Rock with side scan sonar and photographed points of interest from their submersible.

All that remained was the dive itself.

The dive team's preparation paid off, allowing them to complete the job over three eight-hour days. The captain found us a spot on deck where we could watch the action without getting in the way.

Portia and I had seen a lot of each other in the months since she'd announced we'd reached a dead end. I couldn't sleep the night after my aha moment at Forty Steps, when I watched the sailboat take evasive action near Saunder's Ledge. She found me waiting at the door when she arrived at the library the next morning, and she heard me out.

She didn't embrace my plan to hire professional divers to look for evidence of the *Makreel* at Saunder's Ledge, but she didn't dismiss it either.

So I became a regular visitor to the library. My motive at first was to keep Portia interested in pursuing the Black Mine mystery, but since a library is a place for reading, I began thumbing through books and periodicals on my own. Actually reading came later, by fits and starts, and when Portia saw me struggling, she found appropriate books for me to start on. Today people would say I was dyslexic, but back then, I was just a slow reader.

We became good friends. In fact, the better I got to know her, the less I fretted about reading.

By summer, we were seeing each other every day—and not just about books. It took a while for us to realize what was going on, since this was the first real romance either one of us had experienced.

Leo, on one of his periodic visits to Egg Rock, said we were acting like teenagers. By then, that was hardly news to us.

The first dive day dawned sunny, and the fresh snow onshore was thrown into sharp relief by the deep blue ocean. I wondered how Mister Tower would have described the scene.

Late in the day, the crew became visibly excited, and we soon learned they had located part of the keel of a large vessel wedged beneath an overhang on the ledge's east end.

The next day, Portia and I stood by while the divers brought up a total of thirty-nine small objects, including pewter ware, eating utensils, and glass fragments of various sizes.

"That's only the aperitif," remarked the captain, pointing at the haul lying on the deck to dry off.

On the third day, it took hours to free a two-foot section of the keel and ease it to the surface. When it broke free from the water, covered with barnacles and seaweed, everyone cheered.

Portia had arranged for the curator at the maritime museum in Salem to be present. He was a pale, balding gentleman who looked as if he'd been cast for the role, but when the keel broke free from the water, I thought he'd start dancing around the deck. Later, we watched him gently deposit the keel in the back of his van, as if it were a frail patient headed to the hospital.

I proposed to Portia that night.

It wasn't as though we hadn't talked about getting married. I had already bought a nice ring, and I planned to wait another month—Christmas Eve, to be exact—to do it. However, the excitement of the day and the timetable the curator outlined before he drove away got my juices flowing.

Physical examination of the specimen—his words—and initial x-ray results would be ready in a few days, but the all-important carbon dating might take a month or two to come back.

"Why wait?" I asked Portia, and with tears in her eyes, she nodded an emphatic yes.

A couple of days later, the curator called with news that sped his timetable up a bit. The keel's materials (English oak and iron nails) and the construction method (tongue-in-groove) were consistent with a seventeenth-century origin, although only carbon-dating results would be confirmatory.

The x-ray findings were perplexing. A metallic object measuring about eighteen inches long and three inches wide sat lengthwise inside the keel. The curator said he'd never encountered metal reinforcements in ships of that era. "We really don't know why it's there."

However, the metal object, whatever its purpose, might have allowed the segment in which it was imbedded to break off from the rest of the keel, and it had turned out to be just the right size and weight to squeeze into that narrow crevasse deep in Saunder's Ledge.

He invited us to come to the lab the next day to watch him extract the mysterious metal object.

The lab at the Salem museum reminded me of the operating room where I had my gall bladder removed—stainless steel, fluorescent lighting, tiled walls.

The curator wore scrubs and rubber gloves, and he used a small saw and a scalpel for his work.

In minutes, he removed a gray pipe-like metal object that was sealed at both ends.

At that point, he came out to speak with us. "It sounds hollow, making me suspect there's something inside. I can open her up with a welder's torch."

It took a couple of hours of painstaking work to open one end but only seconds to extract a rolled-up paper-like object from the tube.

Portia was shaking. We remained at our place behind the window while the curator and an assistant gently unrolled a sheet of parchment. From where we stood, we could make out the outline of a sailing ship. They laid the sheet on the table and positioned the big overhead camera.

Later, when we entered the curator's office upstairs, a large photograph was lying on a table.

"This is the biggest find of my career," he said quietly. "This will be your copy. We magnified it to twice its size so you can make out some of the detail."

A two-masted ship was the focal point, and it was tilted ominously toward the bow. With a magnifying glass, we could appreciate its intricate square rigging, a lone sailor wedged into the crosstrees of the masthead, and figures of men kneeling on the tilted deck with their hands in prayer and their eyes toward heaven.

*Makreel* was etched on the nearly submerged bow in tiny letters.

Leo drove out to Egg Rock after finishing with his patients. Over the phone, I'd told him what we'd seen and suggested he bring one of his old dictionaries along since there was a lot of writing, and most of it looked like Latin to Portia.

The first thing Leo noticed was how objects lined up. To the ship's left sat Egg Rock, and to its right, the sun was at the horizon. That meant the *Makreel* was going down over Saunder's Ledge at sunrise on a summer morning.

Beneath the water's surface swam schools of fish, and in the distance, a whale spouted water toward the sky, where a pair of angels looked down at the scene.

Pointing at the angels, Leo handed Portia the magnifier. "Take a good look at the darker one."

"Oh my God, he's smiling."

He took the glass from her and moved it over the angel's wing, where something was written: "Hi qui primum legent verba mea sicut hi homines et sicut sui patres utinam in mari moriantur."

"Which means?" Portia asked.

"'Whoever first reads my words in the future will, like these men and like their own fathers, perish in the sea.'"

"It sure helps to have a classicist in the family," I joked.

No one laughed.

The message on the angel's wing took over Portia's life from then on. She agreed she was being irrational, but the fact that both her father and Leo's father had perished in the sea didn't help matters.

Walter's plane had spiraled into the Ionian Sea en route from Athens to Rome, while his brother, Vincent, had drowned in Squimset Bay, only feet from his kitchen door. One morning, Portia had awakened to find him missing and found his body floating face up beside the pier behind their house, his binoculars still around his neck. He'd undoubtedly been out to check the night sky, as he often did, when something happened to him.

With coincidences like that, I found it hard to get her to think about anything else.

When Leo and his family came out for Sunday dinner a couple of weeks after the discovery of the manuscript, no one said a word about the Black Mine. I donated the manuscript to the maritime museum, with the proviso that it not be exhibited during Portia's and Leo's lifetimes.

The wedding went off as scheduled on Christmas Eve afternoon. Father Guido, the chaplain at Saint Kay's Hospital and a close friend of Leo's, performed the simple ceremony in the small side chapel at Saint Lawrence Church.

We're settling into married life quite well, considering. Becoming a couple after so many years of leading single lives is a complicated business. So far, we have transitioned from two houses to one with a minimum of fuss, a good bit of laughter, and no major disagreements.

One bump in the road was the decision to cancel our honeymoon cruise. Portia was convinced she'd spend the whole trip locked in the stateroom with her life jacket within reach.

That was how things stood until about a week ago. Portia had urged me to reconnect with my family, with whom I'd lost contact after my military days.

"They should know that you finally got hitched."

I wrote to my sister at an address I'd saved from a Christmas card sent years earlier but figured I'd hear nothing back. I'd almost forgotten about it, when Portia ran into the house from the mailbox one afternoon.

She nearly tore the letter out of my hands before I finished reading it. When she got to the part about my mom and dad drowning in a ferry accident, all the color drained from her face.

Now Portia and I have another steep hill to climb.

# ℐOHN'S PERIL I

It took Mayland Lowe several days and nights—or maybe it took only hours that seemed like days and nights—to put things together. First, it occurred to him that the bed wasn't his bed. The mattress was too hard, and the pillows were too skimpy. The windows didn't look right either.

He recalled his first time away from home—at age eight in New York with his parents—when he'd awakened to discover that the windows in the hotel room, too, had been the wrong shapes and in the wrong places.

Later, it dawned on him that he was in a hospital room. It was painted institutional beige and had one of those tray-table contraptions at the side of the bed and a TV affixed high on the wall. He tried to detect some telltale hospital smell, such as mercurochrome, iodine, or the faint vanilla smell of adhesive tape, but he couldn't smell a thing.

He slept fitfully. As soon as he closed his eyes, the dreams would start, one after another. One vivid nightmare stuck with him, while the memory of the others melted away as soon as he awoke.

In the nightmare heavy smoke was burning his eyes and choking him. It smelled like the electrical fire he'd experienced a few years earlier at work. A TV monitor had overheated, forcing everyone to evacuate the set during the six o'clock news. As the producer had wisecracked afterward, that was the day they made news instead of reporting it.

He was standing in line. It was obvious no one would make it out alive, but the other passengers politely queued up behind him single file, as if at a supermarket checkout. There was total silence, as if someone had shut off the soundtrack of a movie. Then the guy behind him—no woman he knew could have had such strength—grabbed him by the belt and heaved him through a narrow space. He always woke up the moment he began to fall.

Once he could string a few intelligible words together, he told his sister, Sallie, about the dream.

"It really happened, Mayland."

He was lying flat on his back, attached to a steel structure that must have stretched beyond his feet. He was guessing about his feet, because his head was anchored in place. He thought he could wiggle his toes, but since he couldn't see them, he wasn't sure.

"You broke your neck and both legs when you exited the plane," she explained, "but the doctors say you're not paralyzed. And you have second-degree burns on your back."

His other recollections of the flight were all fragments in high-gloss colors that reminded him of the designs in the kaleidoscope he'd been given as a kid. "The pain meds do that," a nurse told him.

When Sallie informed him it was Monday morning, the twenty-fifth, he couldn't believe it. The last ten days had fallen into a black hole.

The neurologist came in later. He was a tidy-looking man with tortoise-shell-rimmed glasses, a bow tie, and a friendly smile. He stood by the bed and asked all sorts of questions, such as dates, days of the week, and easy math problems that made Mayland worry he'd become an idiot.

The doctor said Mayland had suffered a significant concussion but no permanent brain damage except for loss of smell. He was pleased, he continued, to find Mayland much improved since his last visit on Friday. That sounded fine to Mayland, except for one bothersome detail: he could have sworn he'd never seen the doctor before in his life.

He'd been planning this visit east for months. He looked forward to spending time with his sister, of course, but the new airport intrigued him more than anything else. It wasn't as if he were a student of airports—meteorology was his profession and passion—but Longfellow International was a special case since the entire town of Egg Rock had been leveled to make room for it.

The Longfellow had just about everything the 1960s traveler could dream of. It was the first airport in the world to be built on two islands. The terminal complex, called a mini-city by the press, occupied Little Egg, while the runways, hangars, and airplanes occupied the big island.

A monorail modeled after the one at Disneyland shuttled passengers over the connecting isthmus, where the coast guard lifesaving station once stood.

The terminal complex contained a four-hundred-room hotel; a twenty-five-hundred-space parking garage; smaller versions of old-time Boston restaurants; an indoor shopping center; a full-service post office; banks; Catholic, Protestant, and Jewish chapels; and a moving sidewalk linking all four terminals.

When he last spoke to Sallie over the phone, she joked that he'd be so captivated by the Longfellow that he'd never make it to her apartment.

Then she'd turned angry. "They rob us of our town and expect us to remain silent?"

Mayland had known better than argue the point.

At first, it had looked as if the new airport would be named for a former governor, a military hero, or even a baseball player.

But that had been before the bridge crisis.

The Longfellow Bridge linking Boston and Cambridge had been named for Henry Wadsworth Longfellow, one of the country's most famous poets. Its unique salt-and-pepper towers were as iconic as Faneuil Hall and Fenway Park, so it was headline news when a tour bus carrying retirees to a local racetrack broke through an abutment at the top of the span. The bus hung precariously over the Charles River while rescue crews off-loaded the frightened passengers. Photos of the dangling bus made the front pages of newspapers around the world.

The Longfellow was shut down immediately, causing monumental traffic jams and cutting off all trolley service over the river. However, that was only the beginning of the crisis. Experts determined that the old Longfellow was unsalvageable. The Army Corps of Engineers quickly put a pontoon bridge in place while the old Longfellow was dismantled, and a modern span was constructed in record time.

The new Longfellow was the epitome of contemporary design. The salt-and-pepper towers were gone, in keeping with its sleek, modern profile, but their images were etched onto each of its mercury vapor light poles.

The plan had been to call it the New Longfellow Bridge, but when President Kennedy was assassinated in Dallas, it instantly became the John Fitzgerald Kennedy Memorial Bridge, or the JFK for short.

However, Longfellow wasn't left out in the cold for long.

At the new bridge's dedication, the governor invited a young woman no one recognized to come forward. She stepped to the microphone and read a section from "Paul Revere's Ride." Once the applause died down, the governor introduced Longfellow's great-great-granddaughter.

"I'd love to hear you read that poem again on the day we dedicate the Longfellow International Airport at Egg Rock."

Naming the airport after Egg Rock's most famous resident brought the audience to its feet.

By the end of the Second World War, Boston had outgrown Logan Airfield, but it took years for a replacement to be built. Although planners had their sights on Egg Rock from the start, the townspeople fought back, and they nearly prevailed. However, once the state's highest court upheld the legislature's plan to take the whole town by eminent domain, opposition ebbed away.

Mayland's mother had been a vocal opponent of the move, but by the time the court ruled, Helena Lowe was experiencing memory problems, and she never fully understood what happened. Six months later, she was dead.

"Of a broken heart," Sallie would always say.

Mayland was already working in Minneapolis by the time the court decision came down, but he spent the bulk of his free time back at Egg Rock, helping his sister make the move. Channel 8, the Voice of the Northern Plains, was flexible and sympathetic. The station manager had gone through much the same experience as a kid in Tennessee, where the TVA displaced thousands of families by eminent domain. Mayland's fellow meteorologists adjusted their schedules to give him long weekends for his trips east.

Alone in the old family house, Sallie needed all the help he could give. Pulling up roots would have been a complicated affair for anyone, but for her, with the recent loss of her mother, it was a nightmare. Because she was moving from a ten-room Victorian in Egg Rock to a two-bedroom apartment across the harbor in Dawes, just about everything had to go.

Since the whole town had to go, there was ample guidance from town hall—and the state's new Airport Authority, which townies called the Gestapo—on how to go about it. Meanwhile, many residents discovered more profitable ways to part with their belongings when history buffs, collectors, and junk dealers descended like vultures on the town.

Demolition was scheduled for mid-July, nearly five years after the court decision. Throughout the spring, residents dismantled anything of value that could be carted away, and the pace quickened in the last weeks before the bulldozers were scheduled to arrive.

On Memorial Day, Egg Rockers arrived from all over for the last homecoming. Marie-Francoise Pommier and her son, Denis, traveled the farthest—from Paris, France—for her first trip home in years and his first ever. The parade was the grandest in memory, and the town's landmarks were festooned with bunting.

A brigade of TV trucks rolled in, and townspeople were interviewed on every street corner. The governor and both senators showed up, and Walter Cronkite interviewed F. X. Mulcahy, the town's senior selectman, and the writer Priscilla Crane at the old lifesaving station. Neither pulled any punches.

"This oughta be a wake, not a celebration," the old lobsterman declared.

Priscilla Crane, dressed in widow's weeds, predicted an apocalypse, "reaching far beyond these two little islands and far into the future."

Mayland came again in late June to finish cleaning out the house and to get Sallie settled into her new home.

On the day before Egg Rock was closed down for good, the town was busy a final time. The flags, TV trucks, and dignitaries were gone, and people looked dazed as they wandered their town to say goodbye.

Mayland and Sallie found clusters of old friends at Bear Pond, at Forty Steps, and in front of the library. That neo-Gothic masterpiece, stripped of its leaded windows and tiled roof, was a fitting backdrop for Miss Pettigrew, the town librarian, as she accepted condolences.

They visited the family plot at Evergreen Cemetery before their last trip over the causeway to the mainland. The new cemetery on the far side of Squimset had already been prepared, but the transfer of the remains would be carried out quietly in a series of nightly truck convoys once the town was empty.

The pilot announced that the flight from Minneapolis would be landing at Longfellow International Airport a half hour early on account of a healthy tailwind. Mayland was thrilled to be setting foot in his old hometown again, even though it wasn't even a town anymore. The sooner they touched down, the better.

The stewardesses had to hustle drinks and dinner, but no one seemed to mind. Mayland made a point of looking for the Quabbin Reservoir, created by flooding a valley and obliterating four towns in the process. The pro-airport forces called the Quabbin and the Longfellow triumphs of technology, while others, such as Helena and Sallie Lowe, F. X. Mulcahy, and Priscilla Crane, saw only triumphs of tyranny.

The plane banked sharply off Gloucester for its final approach along the North Shore to the Longfellow. The sun had just set, and lights on the ground were coming on.

That was when Mayland's memory shut down.

Sallie doled out details little by little as he improved, and once she felt he was strong enough, she brought her scrapbook of newspaper clippings to the hospital.

The plane had lost altitude in the last seconds of its approach; crashed into a seawall, which sheared off its landing gear; and slid onto the runway. In the ninety seconds between impact and fire breaking out, the crew had been able to evacuate 29 of the 130 passengers. The remaining 101 passengers and 10 crew members had remained trapped inside. Seven of the 29 rescued had died either en route to the hospital or soon after.

The copilot, the only survivor from the flight deck, had made an observation that was widely quoted: "You get downdrafts all the time, but we'd never seen anything like this. We couldn't pull up one inch."

Mayland pored over the passenger list, as if by focusing on each name, he'd learn who'd saved his life. Finally, Sallie put her foot down.

"Why torture yourself? Since you were the last one out, there's no one left to thank."

Mayland spent nearly four months in the hospital and another month recuperating at Sallie's apartment in Dawes.

Channel 8 assured him that no matter how long it took, his old job would be waiting for him. Meanwhile, they sent a reporter and cameraman east to get updates on his condition for the folks in Minneapolis.

Mayland soon had a fan club, and the Nielson ratings for the six o'clock news went through the roof.

Priscilla Crane invited Mayland and Sallie to visit. They made a date for the day before his scheduled flight home.

Priscilla, Helena Lowe, and F. X. Mulcahy had been on the front lines in the struggle to save the town. Those who wondered why Priscilla, a semi-reclusive writer, had joined the others weren't aware that years earlier, she'd walked the picket lines during the Squimset shoe strike.

Priscilla and Mulcahy became in-your-face protesters, while Helena stayed in the background, writing letters to newspapers and attending behind-the-scenes meetings with legislative leaders.

But even Priscilla's most fervent supporters felt she had gone too far when she called the governor a weasel during a televised news conference.

For an encore, she sneaked back into the abandoned town and chained herself to the great elm in front of town hall the day the bulldozers arrived, and spent overnight in a local jail for her efforts.

Mayland wondered if she'd ever mellowed.

Priscilla's new home sat at the top of Sagamore Hill in Squimset. She led her guests into the living room, where tea had been set out.

The view was breathtaking, with Big and Little Egg Rock stretched out beyond the floor-to-ceiling windows. Traffic streamed across the causeway while planes, in a kind of aeronautical ballet, landed and took off.

A half-completed painting of the same view stood on an easel. Mayland adjusted his glasses to get a better look.

"It's been sitting there like that for months. My friend Gretchen drops in to fiddle with it once in a while, but she can't seem to get it right."

It was a writer's room. Bookshelves lined the walls, and a handsome double-pedestal desk and plush armchair sat before the windows.

Four arrowheads in a glass case caught Mayland's eye.

"I rescued them from Egg Rock, but it took me decades of surface hunting to come up with that much. I know there's a treasure trove of them out there, but they're lost now, like so many other Egg Rock secrets."

"That reminds me, Priscilla. Is your book about the town still selling?" Mayland had his own autographed copy at home in Minneapolis.

"Believe it or not, *Forty Steps* is in its fifth printing! My editor keeps bugging me to update it with some new stories now that the town is dead and buried, but I'm not sure my heart is in it."

Over tea, they caught up on each other's lives. Priscilla filled them in on her nephew, Jacob, whom she'd adopted after his parents were killed.

"He's practically grown up now—a senior in college with a serious girlfriend."

Sallie talked about her move to Dawes, and the two women agreed that downsizing was a torture. Mayland spoke about his life as a meteorologist, describing the day he'd watched a tornado sweep through a small Minnesota town, flattening everything on one side of a street and leaving the other side untouched. They talked about Egg Rock, the fun they'd had as kids, and that sort of thing until Priscilla changed the subject.

"I was sitting right here, when there was a horrendous flash. By the time I focused the binoculars, I could see that a plane was burning on one of the runways. In minutes, the causeway was clogged with emergency vehicles."

Sallie joined in. "I was frosting a welcome-home cake for Mayland when I heard the sirens. When they didn't quiet down, I realized that it probably meant something had happened at the airport. Even then, my only worry was that Mayland's cab would be delayed, and dinner would be ruined."

Priscilla refilled their cups and changed the subject again.

"If I ever get around to updating *Forty Steps*, it will be to tell the world about John's Peril."

Mayland had heard of John's Peril before, but he knew only that it was one of those quirky places in Egg Rock, like the Black Mine, Bear Pond, or Curlew Beach.

"At the northeast corner of the big island, there's a cliff about an eighth of a mile long. The runway where your flight crashed ends along the midpoint of that cliff. The topography is totally changed now, since it's been built up a good hundred feet for the Longfellow's longest runway.

"In colonial days, a farmer named John Breed was surveying the meadow above the cliff for grazing land. When he got too close to the edge, he lost control of his cart and was barely able to save himself and his oxen by unhitching the cart and allowing it to tumble into the sea. Breed, by all accounts, was a cautious man, which made people wonder whether something beyond his control had taken place. Of course, it was a time when superstition played a big role in people's lives. Around then, so-called witches were being crushed by stones and hanged a few miles up the coast in Salem. So it's no surprise that folks wondered if the land had been cursed by the Indians and if Breed had been given a warning. In any case, John's Peril became a no-man's-land. For generations, no one would set foot there."

She pointed to a portrait on the wall behind her. "Meet Winnipurket, the sachem of the Naumkeag tribe. It's believed that he lived on this hill when the first Europeans arrived."

He was a dark-skinned young man with a prominent nose, a high forehead, and jet-black hair pulled back severely into two long braids. His large, deep-set eyes looked sad and defiant.

"Of course, we have no idea what Winnipurket looked like, so my friend Gretchen got a local boy to sit for her, and she let her imagination take over."

"Handsome fellow," said Sallie.

"Winnipurket and his wife and brothers died of smallpox. Smallpox was unknown to the Native Americans before it was imported by the ships carrying the new settlers. And it hit them hard. More than three-quarters of the native population here died in the first outbreak.

"Here's where the story gets interesting. You see, the Naumkeag burial ground was in Egg Rock, and it's likely Winnipurket and his family were buried there. No one knows where the burial ground is exactly, but they favored flat land with a view of the sunrise, like John's Peril."

"And about a thousand other places on the island."

"Yes, Sallie, but I'm convinced the burial ground was at John's Peril. It makes perfect sense. Besides, I have proof."

Sallie looked upward with a "What's next?" expression, but Priscilla didn't seem to notice.

"Your flight number was 1636, Mayland, and 1636 was the year Winnipurket and his family died."

Mayland, who had wondered if Priscilla had mellowed, was now convinced she'd lost her mind. He tried to lighten the conversation by asking about some other exiles, such as the Mulcahy family and Clara Junior, who had taken over her mother's grocery store.

"She's actually Clara the Fourth," Priscilla replied. "That little store was started by Junior's great-grandmother, also a Clara. Egg Rock's only matriarchy."

She then asked if they remembered Dennis Tierney.

Mayland nodded. "How could I forget him? We made fun of him behind his back when he took our school pictures from his wheelchair. Kids can be so cruel."

"Exile has been extra hard on him. Shut out of that ingeniously designed house, he's like a fish out of water. He's living in a rest home now, and I hear he's so despondent that he's refusing to see visitors."

Priscilla got to her feet and walked to the windows. "Aren't you afraid to fly again? I know I'd be."

"I guess it's the old story of getting back on the horse. Remember, I'm a weatherman. Every time I'm up there, I get such a kick out of watching the clouds and the fronts and even getting bounced around by a storm once in a while. I can't give that up."

"I tried to get Mayland to take the train home or take the train to New York and fly home from there. The way I see it, setting foot on the ruins of our beautiful town is a sacrilege!"

Priscilla gave Sallie a nod and tapped on the glass with such force that Mayland thought it would crack. "The place is doomed. I have dreams about the islands getting blown to smithereens by an atomic bomb or being inundated by an epic flood. The view breaks my heart little by little every day, but I need to be up here so I can record what happens next."

Driving back to Dawes that evening, Mayland wondered how soon Priscilla, like Dennis Tierney, would be put away.

"Do you remember what Priscilla predicted on Egg Rock's last Memorial Day?"

Mayland shrugged.

"An apocalypse. Priscilla may be losing her mind, but there can be a thin line between madness and prophecy."

Mayland took an early cab to the airport. Sallie promised to watch from her kitchen window to make sure he got off safely.

When they reached the causeway, he had the taxi stop at the Egg Rock Monument. During their visit to Sagamore Hill, Priscilla Crane had urged him to have a look.

The obelisk, the kind one might see in the Civil War section in a cemetery, bore a simple inscription:

> These two islands made up the town of Egg Rock.
> Visited by the Vikings in the 11th century, settled in
> 1630, incorporated in 1853, disenfranchised in 1963.
> Let us never forget those who loved this place.

At the airport, Mayland ordered the Patriot's Premium Breakfast at the New Union Oyster House, a replica of the original restaurant in Boston. He had another pot of coffee brought to the table while he watched planes take off and get swallowed by the high overcast. Before draining his last cup, he downed the Valium tablet the doctor had prescribed for the flight.

"This should take the edge off," the doctor had said. "The first flight after what you've been through should be the hardest."

The hilly, big island, smoothed out by hundreds of tons of fill, looked as flat as a tabletop. He tried to pinpoint the location of the vets' club and Whitecaps, his favorite house in Egg Rock, but there were no reference points left to work with. The only places he could be sure of were the rock itself offshore, its newly installed landing lights icy blue in the morning gloom, and John's Peril.

He'd been able to book his favorite seat—and the one he considered the safest—at a window five rows behind the wing.

As they taxied to the west end of the airport, he could make out Sallie's apartment building on the far side of Squimset Harbor, and he wondered if she indeed was watching.

The plane made a wide turn, righted itself on the runway, and accelerated. Takeoff had always been one of Mayland's favorite moments. The sensation of the powerful engines picking up speed and thrusting his body back always had an erotic feel. Despite the circumstances, he felt remarkably calm.

Suddenly, something went wrong. He pitched forward, striking his head on the tray table in front of him. Luggage toppled out of the overhead racks; people around him screamed; and in seconds, the plane veered off the runway and bounced onto the grass alongside, traveling so fast and bucking so violently that he pictured the whole fuselage breaking up.

He focused on the scene outside, hoping that by concentrating on the landscape flying by, he could magically slow the plane down. Just then, the window darkened, and another man stared back at him. His shiny black hair was pulled back severely over his high forehead, and his deep-set eyes were sad and defiant.

Sallie sat frozen in her chair once the sirens started.

When the phone rang, she prayed that whoever it was would go away, but it rang and rang until she picked up.

Priscilla sounded calm and self-assured. Sallie could hear a radio in the background.

"They're saying something about a sinkhole at the airport."

The sinkhole made headlines all over the country. Walter Cronkite featured the story on the evening news.

Reports indicated that a morning flight to Minneapolis was taxiing for takeoff, when a traffic controller noticed a black mark, like a giant inkblot, forming at the far end of the runway. Thinking quickly, he instructed the pilot to abort. After skidding off the runway, the plane came to rest only a few feet from a steep cliff at the edge of the island. Had it fallen into the sinkhole, which by then had grown to twenty feet across and close to a hundred feet deep, or over the cliff into the sea, all on board likely would have been lost. Fortunately, only one passenger on board died, of an apparent heart attack. It was a harrowing experience for the others, who came away with bumps, bruises, and a few broken bones. There was an unconfirmed report that the man who died had survived the crash at the Longfellow six months earlier.

Sinkholes, it was reported, could open up over weakened or hollowed-out earth. They most commonly occurred on top of old mines or places where the earth had been drastically altered, as in the case of the new Longfellow International Airport.

Days later, Priscilla Crane telephoned her editor to let him know she had no intention of updating her book after all.

"Why not? With Egg Rock in the news again, an updated *Forty Steps* could be a Book of the Month Club selection, or at least an alternate."

"Didn't you hear about the election? Now that I've been sworn in as Egg Rock's mayor, I intend to restore the town to the paradise it once was. There will be no time for writing foolish books!"

# $\mathcal{J}$OHN'S PERIL II

It took Mayland Lowe several days and nights—or maybe it took only hours that seemed like days and nights—to put things together.

He was in a hospital.

Sallie was sitting next to the bed when he woke up.

"Where's Ramona?" were his first words.

In the next few hours, as his head got clearer, Sallie told him everything in her usual methodical fashion, stopping every few minutes to make sure he was absorbing the information.

There had been a fire. Mayland and Ramona had been the only ones in the house at the time, and they both had gotten out. Actually, they'd jumped. Otherwise, they would have been burned alive.

The second floor of Whitecaps was a good thirty feet off the ground, but the ancient rhododendron bushes surrounding the house had broken their fall.

The facts, in order of importance, were the following:

- Ramona was in intensive care but expected to survive.
- Mayland had two broken legs, a concussion, and second-degree burns to his back.
- The fire had been intentionally set.
- The house had suffered extensive damage but was basically intact. Workmen were already making repairs.

Later, Sallie brought in a scrapbook she'd made of newspaper clippings about the fire and the investigation. There had been no arrests, and apparently, the police had no suspects.

It was a week before Mayland and Ramona got to see each other. Rolling Mayland to his wife's room down the hall, Sallie wondered what was going through his head. He and Ramona had drifted apart—she knew they would go days without saying a word to each other. However, she also knew Mayland would never abandon her.

A police detective interviewed them while they were still in the hospital. Her first question was about any enemies they might have.

"Enemies?" Ramona shot back, annoyed that anyone could suggest such an absurd idea.

"Think back," the detective persisted. "Some people hold on to their grudges forever. And grudges can be handed down for generations."

It didn't take long for Mayland to realize how many lives he'd entered, however briefly, and how many opportunities he'd had to offend.

A "fan" letter from years before came to mind. A viewer's daughter had planned a garden wedding on a summer Saturday afternoon. Mayland had failed to predict thunderstorms on his Friday forecast, and the ceremony had been a disaster. The letter was filled with obscenities, and in place of a signature, the writer had drawn an elaborate gallows.

---

🎋

They didn't make it back home for three months. Even then, the first thing Mayland noticed was the smell. It reminded him of a fire that had broken out on the set years earlier. As the producer wisecracked at the time, that was the day they made news instead of reporting it.

Ramona didn't notice it.

The fire had started on the kitchen stairs, where someone had ignited a pile of gasoline-soaked rags. Since they never locked their doors, anyone could have gotten into the house.

Sallie had the formal dining room converted into a temporary bedroom since it would be months before they'd be strong enough to use the stairs to the second floor.

But they never made it upstairs, even to have a look. Mayland couldn't bear the thought of returning to the room where they'd nearly died, and Ramona didn't seem to care one way or another.

Coworkers filled in for Mayland, and the station hired a new member of Boston's Channel 8 Weather Team to take up the slack.

Mayland clung to the idea of getting back to work, until the evening the station's owner came to Egg Rock with the bad news.

Mayland, known as the dean of forecasters, had kept a rigorous schedule right up to the night of the fire. He gave his early morning "Land and Sea" forecast seven days a week, broadcasting from his weather station in a converted widow's walk at the top of the house. Then he drove to the studio in town for a series of early evening TV weather segments five nights a week.

"Think of this as an opportunity to get off the treadmill and pursue other interests" was how the owner put it.

The problem was, Mayland had no other interests.

Ramona acted as if the fire had never happened, spending each day seated ramrod straight on a kitchen chair, watching the Game Show Network. In the old days, she'd tuned in to one of Mayland's forecasts for a few minutes each day, but that had been the only time she'd watched. She called TV "a failed experiment," and she spoke with some authority. Before they married, she'd hosted *Good Morning, Ladies*, one of Channel 8's earliest programs.

One of her first guests had been Mayland Lowe, the station's dashing young weatherman.

†

Rabomis Shortledge had been raised in northern New Hampshire by an Abenaki mother and Yankee father. Only when she got to Boston did she become Ramona, the closest English name she could come up with.

Mayland was knocked off his feet the first time he saw her. She wasn't pretty in the conventional sense, especially back in the 1950s, the era of bouffant blondes, but she was the most alluring woman he had ever met.

She was dark-skinned and had a prominent nose, a high forehead, and jet-black hair pulled back severely. But what struck him most were her eyes—deep-set and inscrutable.

He asked her what her name meant.

"Rabomis was a famous sachem, a tribal chief—a rare woman in a man's job."

Their wedding was a major social event covered by all the Boston newspapers and a phalanx of cameramen from Channel 8. After a honeymoon in Europe, they moved to Egg Rock and started life as Boston's version of royalty.

As one columnist wrote, "Mayland and Ramona are as well known in these parts as the Pilgrims, Paul Revere, and Ted Williams all rolled into one."

Ramona cut back her schedule at the station, appearing only to host special events, such as the annual Boston Marathon and the Fourth of July concert.

That gave her time to keep house, cook, and tend a vegetable garden on the grassy knoll outside the kitchen, where she planted rows of corn, squash, and beans the way her mother had when Ramona was little. That first garden hadn't been a hobby, as this one was. Her mother had worked it every day in season and gotten Ramona and her brother to help with weeding, picking, and canning as soon as they were old enough. Looking back, she realized that without it, they would have starved.

The day she planted her first corn crop, her hoe struck a hard object, and she bent over to find an arrowhead. By the end of the day, she'd collected more than fifty.

She contacted her neighbor, a woman named Priscilla Crane, who got excited on the phone and hurried over to have a look.

Priscilla, a well-known writer, had spent years as a surface hunter. Even in Egg Rock, a small place, she'd been able to find a few arrowheads, but her greatest find had been on the grassy headland above Forty Steps, where she'd come across a boulder with a round scooped-out area on its top that made it look like an oversize birdbath. People had walked by that rock for hundreds of years without realizing it was a mortar that Indian women had used to make flour by pounding dried kernels of corn.

With Priscilla's help, Ramona discovered that Whitecaps had been the site of an ancient campsite. It was ideally situated, on high, flat south-facing ground. In the process of enlarging the garden, they uncovered adzes and gouge scrapers, sinkers for fishing lines, and weights for their nets. When Mayland had a garage built, workmen uncovered an enormous pile of clam, oyster, and mussel shells.

"Wow! A midden!" Priscilla exclaimed. "Those folks did some serious eating!"

Later, the two would-be archeologists started digging at a spot on the north side of the island called John's Peril. Priscilla had long suspected it was the site of a native burial ground. "I knew it. I knew it," she muttered as they unearthed a treasure trove of stone tools, weapons, and jewelry.

The day the John's Peril Burial Ground was dedicated as a national historic site, representatives of Native American tribes from all over New England celebrated with music and dancing. Ramona, clothed in ceremonial bearskins, watched from the seat of honor.

Soon after Mayland and Ramona were finally released from the hospital, Mayland got a phone call from Priscilla Crane. The call came as a surprise, since they hadn't exchanged more than a hello since Ramona and Priscilla's archeological period years earlier.

She'd become a recluse, sending a black woman out for errands. But she wanted to drop by.

Priscilla had to be about ninety, he calculated as he welcomed her at the door. She had visibly shrunken since he'd last seen her.

She wasted no time in getting to why she'd come. "I saw the man who lit the fire."

She'd been on Curlew Beach, and since the tide was in, she had to stand just inside the fence separating the beach from the road. At her age, she continued, sleep had become a will-o'-the wisp, so she was apt to be out and about at night.

The sound of someone trotting along the road had startled her.

"My eyes aren't the greatest," she admitted, "but when he passed under the streetlight, I got a good look."

The man was probably Mayland's age, she added, but he was short and stooped and wore a cap pulled down to hide his face.

"He was so close I could nearly reach through the fence and touch him. The sleeve on his left arm had been pinned back at the elbow. As soon as he saw me, he sprinted away and disappeared."

"Did you call the police?"

"I don't trust the police."

"If I talk to them—"

"Go ahead! We can't have a firebug on the loose around here."

It didn't take long for the police to arrest Stephen Wadsworth for arson and attempted murder.

Mayland and Sallie remembered the name well.

Mayland and Stephen Wadsworth had crossed paths decades earlier. Actually, "crossing paths" was overstating things, since they'd never actually met.

After serving as a weather observer in Korea, Mayland wrote letters to dozens of TV stations across the country, inquiring about weather-forecasting positions.

And received zero responses.

He finally landed a job at the Westinghouse plant in Squimset, building jet engines, and as time went on, he put his dreams aside and concentrated on supporting his widowed mother and Sallie, who was still in school. A year or so later, a station in Minnesota tried to reach him by phone. Helena Lowe took the message while he was at work, and by the time she remembered to tell him about it, the job had been filled. She was already having memory problems by then, so he never allowed himself to get angry about the missed opportunity.

The following winter, he came down with a stomach bug and took the first day off from work in all the time he'd been at the plant. That turned out to be the day he answered the phone himself. The manager of Channel 8 in Boston was on the line. Their regular weatherman had taken ill, and they needed a temporary replacement. He had kept Mayland's letter, and he invited him to come to the station for an interview. Full of paregoric, Mayland drove into town in a daze. He somehow sounded smart enough to be hired and was on the air early the next morning.

He was an instant success. Fan mail poured in. Listeners wrote about how enthusiastic he was, and Channel 8's Nielsen ratings went through the roof. When Steve Wadsworth, the former weatherman at Channel 8, was arrested soon afterward, Mayland was hired full-time.

The story of Stephen Wadsworth's arraignment on a morals charge appeared in the newspapers, accompanied by a picture of him arriving at court.

Sallie gasped when she saw it. "The poor man—he has only half an arm! Did you know that, Mayland?"

Mayland shook his head. For years his predecessor had positioned himself in front of the weather map so that the missing forearm never appeared on TV.

From time to time she'd wondered what had become of Stephen Wadsworth.

Now she knew.

Sallie moved into Whitecaps to help out since Ramona kept going downhill. Ramona's shiny black hair turned white seemingly overnight.

She sat in front of the TV every waking hour, became mute, stopped eating, and died less than a year after the fire.

Mayland was more relieved than anything else. Long before the fire, the royal couple had become little more than a marketing tool for Channel 8.

They had no children. Ramona had gone through three pregnancies but miscarried each time. After that, she lost interest in everything—and everyone—except her vegetable garden. One day Mayland overheard her out there amid the corn stalks, talking to her ancestors.

She began sipping from vodka bottles stashed all over the property. Then she appeared on the set drunk and never worked again.

Mayland consulted a psychiatrist. He was a tidy-looking man with tortoise-shell-rimmed glasses, a bow tie, and a friendly smile. He prescribed pills, but Ramona threw them away and refused to go back.

Mayland kept going for years after the fire, as much to please his sister, Sallie, as anything else. He was haunted, he kept telling her, by what might have been.

"If Mother had told me about that phone call, I would have ended up in Minneapolis. Ramona would never have been part of our lives, and there would have been no fire."

"But Ramona saved Egg Rock from the airport. Remember how the authorities coveted our town but backed off on account of John's Peril? If Ramona and Priscilla Crane hadn't unearthed all those arrowheads, they would have sent in the bulldozers."

"Get real, Sallie. An airport instead of this paradise? Better a snowball's chance in hell!"

# $\mathcal{V}$IOLA'S TREASURE

The Egg Rock Public Library was Viola Pettigrew's second home. Perhaps it had been predestined, since the house where she was born sat on the same block.

But that was hardly the way she had planned things.

She was finishing her studies at the normal school in Salem and already had her teaching  certificate when the librarian job unexpectedly opened up. With the Depression grinding on endlessly, she'd had no luck finding a teaching job, so when her mother urged her to apply, she did—more out of desperation than anything else.

Days after graduation, she sat before the board of selectmen for an interview, and they hired her on the spot. The board seemed oblivious to the fact that Viola was only twenty-one and, except for being a first-class bookworm, had no experience.

There were other applicants, they told her, but a comment by one of the selectmen explained their choice: "We prefer to hire one of our own."

Viola had been in her new job for less than a week when the chief librarian from Squimset dropped by. Alice McBrien had been raised in Egg Rock, and when she saw this girl in way over her head, she made a point of dropping by whenever she could in order to show Viola how to run a library.

They became lifelong friends, members of what Alice called the "bookish sisterhood."

Viola was still getting her feet wet, when she made an extraordinary discovery.

Her friend Alice urged her to make the stacks a priority. Mrs. Samson, Viola's predecessor, had continued a tradition that stretched back to the opening of the Gothic Revival library building around the turn of the century.

Nothing was ever thrown away.

On the top level of the stacks, Viola stumbled on a room she'd never known existed, since piles of books obscured its trapdoor-like entrance. It looked like a closet until she pulled away a few volumes to find the space extending under the entire roof of the building. Books had been tossed in there haphazardly, with many heavier ones landing on top, so when she removed just one, piles began to shift.

She could picture the banner headline in the *Squimset Sentinel*: "Egg Rock Librarian Crushed by Tons of Books."

It was like cleaning out the family attic, where next to a bag of discarded Christmas wrappings, you might come across Grandmother's wedding portrait. It wasn't as if one could back a truck into the parking lot and toss the whole sorry mess out the window.

Digging deeper, she discovered whole private libraries that had been dumped there. Egg Rock had been a popular summer resort with Boston's upper crust in the 1800 s, but the big summer cottages had long since been abandoned.

Alice showed her how to group the books.

First were the obvious throwaways: duplicates and badly damaged volumes of no significance.

Next were books of limited or specialized value, which she could offer to other libraries or dealers or display for sale on the large table in the lobby downstairs.

Finally, there were the keepers—books and papers she had to find room for.

It took her months to remove every book and determine its fate. She was giving the place a last inspection with a flashlight and worrying about the space filling up again, when something caught her eye: a glimmer of yellow.

Stuck between floorboards in a far corner was a rectangular object about the size of a business envelope. It was lemon colored, streaked with grime, and held together by a crimson cord. She picked the package up with great care, the way a doctor would handle a just-delivered infant, and slipped it into her bag.

After work that evening, she sat down at the dining room table, untied the cord, and discovered a treasure.

It was a sheaf of twenty-one letters—she counted right away—all addressed in the same hand to Mr. H. W. Longfellow in Egg Rock, Massachusetts, and all signed by Emily Dickinson. Dickinson wrote about her life in Amherst and included early drafts of some of her best-known work and, amazingly, nine poems Viola didn't recognize. The next morning at the library, she confirmed her suspicions: none of the nine had ever been published.

Longfellow's cottage in Egg Rock had burned to the ground in the late nineteenth century. Everyone assumed the house had been a total loss, with nothing salvaged.

Viola had discovered Emily Dickinson in school. Unlike anything she'd ever read, the poems were profoundly unsettling, with their uncompromising view of life. Once she learned they shared the same birthday, the tenth of December, she began thinking of Emily as her spiritual twin. They led parallel lives—a hundred years apart—as spinsters in small New England towns, observing, imagining, doubting, and hoping. They were set apart, of course, by Emily's genius and courage. Viola was no poet, but even if she had been, she would never have been bold enough to share her innermost thoughts with the world.

The newly discovered poems were like invitations to an

exhilarating and terrifying place where the usual rules didn't apply—where the essential questions of love, faith, beauty, sadness, loneliness, and death were unencumbered by convention and tradition.

She was always one to follow the rules, but these outrageous poems emboldened her. This treasure, she decided, would be for her eyes only.

Viola's father, a deeply private man, had shown her his hiding place days before he died. He'd seemed reluctant to tell his young daughter, but with her mother already sickly and moody, he'd had no one else to confide in. He'd explained how his own father had hollowed out the ornate mantelpiece in the parlor and fitted it with a spring-activated panel. "Press it like this and ..."

Once inside the hiding place, the treasure stayed put—except for every tenth of December. With Mother in bed for the night, Viola would read the nine poems aloud by candlelight.

In later years, with the house to herself, she made the celebration more elaborate, with a dinner of roast duck and angel cake, as meticulously described in one of the letters.

With the passing years, Viola became a respected librarian, a fixture in Egg Rock, and, finally, an institution. By the time she considered retiring, she was the only librarian the townspeople had ever known, having outlasted dozens of boards of selectmen.

For the past year, she'd found herself looking backward instead of forward. Milestones, such as giving up the only real job she'd ever had, she understood, were an opportunity to take stock, tidy up, and leave the fewest loose ends possible.

She'd never married but couldn't decide whether to regret or celebrate that fact. Unlike other children, she'd spent little time playing with dolls and pretending to be a mother. Her parents had not been a particularly happy couple but had not been markedly unhappy either. They simply put one foot in front of the other every day because there was no choice.

She planned to inform the board right after her seventy-fourth birthday to give them a year to find a replacement. During her professional life, library science had indeed become a science, and there promised to be many capable applicants for the position.

People she hadn't seen in years started dropping by, as if they'd gotten wind of her campaign to tidy up. They reminded her of characters in a sprawling Victorian novel who, after being absent for hundreds of pages, made cameo appearances near the end.

A gentleman she hadn't thought much about for ages walked into the library one afternoon. Decades earlier, he'd actually proposed to her. A prominent lawyer and recent widower, he'd lived in Boston with his two small children back then. When Viola asked for time to consider his proposal, he'd seemed offended by her hesitation and withdrawn his offer. It turned out that he never did remarry, and his children were now grown, with families of their own. He came to apologize, as he put it, for his long-ago brusque behavior, but she sensed that neither of them regretted her hesitation.

Priscilla Crane dropped by with her adopted son, Jacob, a linguistics professor in California. He came to thank her at long last, he said, for borrowing countless foreign-language books from other libraries on his behalf when he was a high school student.

Then Joey Steele showed up. She'd always wondered what had happened to the troubled young veteran, who'd left Egg Rock without saying goodbye to anyone. She had offered him a smorgasbord of books on war all the way from Homer to Hemingway, and he'd gobbled every one up.

"Joey!" she exclaimed the minute he came through the door. The tilt of his head, as if he were listening to a far-off voice, gave him away. He placed a small object on the counter, gave Viola a formal bow, and disappeared before she could utter another word. She looked down to discover a delicately crafted silver brooch depicting a dove in flight with an olive branch in its beak. With a magnifying glass, she could make out the tiny letters *JS* on the back.

From what she could learn, there were no other sightings of Joey Steele that day, just as there hadn't been any in the previous forty years.

From that moment on, the silver brooch became as much a part of her daily attire as the reading glasses hanging by a cord around her neck.

That left the matter of the nine unpublished poems. For years, she'd kept the secret to herself, fearful that both her mother and her friend Alice would have been scandalized by what she had done.

The only person she'd ever told was Father Ralph, the priest at Saint Lawrence Church, and it had taken years for her to do that.

One day she stepped into the confessional without the intention of doing any such thing, but the words tumbled out as if someone had thrown a switch.

In a small town like Egg Rock, confession was not a completely anonymous affair. If you had something too private or too embarrassing for the priest's ears, you could go into Boston, where Saint Anthony's Shrine had confessionals running practically twenty-four hours a day, and the priest had no idea who you were.

It wasn't that Father Ralph was consciously violating the seal of confession. He just had a habit of insinuating things. He had been at Saint Lawrence's so long that the townies forgave his shenanigans as if he were a beloved but eccentric uncle.

An outsider would have sworn he'd been born and raised in Egg Rock. Like the natives, he even kept a small boat and a handful of well-positioned lobster traps.

Father Ralph had advised Viola to return the items to the library, and that was how things had stood for more than a year. He continued to give her absolution but brought the subject up gently at the end of each weekly confession. On occasion, he referred to her "continuing sin" obliquely in conversations with her outside of the confessional.

Emily's 150th birthday was to be the grandest party yet, but as the time drew near, Viola changed course and decided to make it her most modest—and her last. Angel cake and the readings would be about it.

Then she'd summon the courage to part with her treasure, although it would be like cutting off her right arm. She'd tuck the poems exactly where she'd found them, snug between the floorboards in the room above the stacks.

It was all about tidying up.

That would put an end to Father Ralph's appeals to her conscience—but that wasn't the whole of it. At a recent confession, he said she was committing two sins by not only stealing but by finding pleasure in the poems, which he referred to as "scandalous works."

"Not unlike an addiction to pornography," he added quietly.

Perhaps she'd "find" the letters again, or her successor—or her successor's successor—would find them, but she hadn't thought that part through yet. In any case, they would be safe and, once discovered, would provide a needed windfall. Budget cuts meant deferred maintenance, and lately, the roof was starting to leak, necessitating the strategic placement of buckets around the building during heavy storms.

For the world of literary scholarship, nine newly discovered poems by one of the country's most celebrated writers would be a godsend sure to make the tiny Egg Rock Public Library world famous.

She pictured herself, years into retirement, in charge of the Emily Dickinson Collection housed in the spectacular new wing of the library.

She lowered the lights, blew out the fifteen candles (a ten-to-one ratio, she'd reasoned), while the letters, still tied with their crimson cord, sat before her on the table.

Just then, she heard a buzzing sound, as if an insect were loose in the room. She couldn't believe that a mosquito could be alive in the middle of December. She reached for the lamp to get a better look, but it suddenly grew too dark to find the switch.

Father Ralph heard the call on his police scanner.

The officer let him in right away. Viola was seated in her favorite chair with a puzzled look he'd seen many times on the faces of folks who'd met a sudden death.

*You do not know the day or the hour.*

It was the look he hoped to see. Faces grimacing in pain or open-mouthed in terror were the worst. Viola had been blessed.

He had his bag with him, but since he wouldn't be administering the sacrament of the sick, he set it on the table in front of her.

He could never get comfortable with the new bland and business-like terminology. The ancient words *viaticum* (sustenance for the last journey) and *extreme unction* (the final application of sacred oils) emphasized the solemnity and mystery of dying. Besides, his fellow seminarians had been in the habit of calling the sacrament of the sick the SOS.

After giving his blessing and reciting the Our Father, which the young policeman in the room tentatively joined, he carefully picked up the bag and made his way back to Saint Lawrence's.

Saint Lawrence's was so packed that latecomers were forced to stand shoulder to shoulder along the back of the church and along the sides, in front of the Stations of the Cross. Usually, the only time Father Ralph witnessed such a turnout was at a funeral for the young, where endless lines of shell-shocked teenagers filed in, or, at least in the old days, when the huge family of the departed jammed the pews. In the past decade, even Christmas and Easter had attracted only half the number who came to Viola Pettigrew's send-off. He wondered how many would show up when his time came.

*Things turned out for the best,* he said to himself. Viola's life had been so intertwined with the library that he'd worried how she'd survive retirement. The way he saw it, God had granted Viola a full life and a merciful death.

*But why?* he wondered. Rewarding an unrepentant thief struck him as still another entry on the long list of God's inscrutable ways.

He'd handled the poem problem skillfully, he felt, smiling at how neat a play on words *handled* was. The packet of letters had been sitting on the dining table, inviting him to pick it up. The dumb-as-a-post cop, who couldn't even recite the Our Father, hadn't seen him slip his fingers around it when he picked up the viaticum bag.

Seated in the rectory office the day after the funeral, he placed the packet before him the way Viola must have a few days earlier.

In confession after confession, he'd urged her to return the packet to the library. Viola could have simply put it back where she'd found it, but the attic room she'd described in such detail was off-limits to the public.

Now it was his problem.

Studying the lemon-yellow envelopes bound by a crimson cord, he watched them waver before his eyes like the air above a chimney on a winter day.

The doctor called the phenomenon his migraine aura. "Auras are like fingerprints. Every patient has his own version."

The shimmering, as Father Ralph called it, lasted about a minute. After that, he'd experience about an hour of intense mental clarity before the headache took over.

Ever since his first attack decades earlier, he'd wondered whether migraine auras were the clairvoyant saints' little secret, giving them moments when the veil was lifted and they saw through a glass clearly.

In any event, it seemed a propitious time to untie the cord and take a look.

An hour later, he nestled the packet inside a spare money bag, locked it in the safe, lowered the shades, and stretched out on the sofa.

Just before the pounding in his right temple—it was always the right—overwhelmed him, he made a decision: Viola's treasure wouldn't be going anywhere.

Raoul Levesque, raised in Salem, had transferred to the archdiocesan seminary midway through his freshman year in college. By then, he'd anglicized his name to Ralph Bishop, leading to a running joke that he was predestined to be elevated to the rank of bishop one day.

The seminary rector, a bishop himself, wasn't amused. The Bishop-becoming-bishop jokes, he intoned, were an affront to the magisterium and to the Holy Spirit, who ultimately guided such weighty issues as episcopal appointments.

Father Ralph's Egg Rock assignment came during his twenty-fifth year as a priest. He'd spent years as an assistant in parishes south of Boston, but with his widowed mother still living in the family home, he'd long pestered the personnel board for a North Shore position.

Once assigned to Egg Rock, he pestered the personnel board to allow him to stay put each time his term ended. One review years back had been complicated by ambiguity regarding a parishioner's bequest, but with the assistance of an old classmate of Ralph's at the chancery, the matter had been quickly resolved.

On the eve of Father Ralph's seventy-fifth birthday, the expected letter from the archbishop's office arrived, offering blessings and congratulations and summoning him to a meeting at the chancery to discuss his future.

At the meeting days later, the archbishop was in high spirits, telling Ralph a silly nun joke and assuring him that he could stay on indefinitely.

So it continued to be business as usual, with Father Ralph tending to the spiritual needs of his Egg Rock parish. That meant saying one daily Mass and two on Sunday; officiating at weddings and funerals; making sick visits; overseeing Sunday school, adult Bible study, and the food pantry; hosting AA, a bereavement group, and a mother's prayer group; and being available for unexpected crises. He had been doing the job for so long that the tasks weren't nearly as burdensome as they might have appeared to an outsider, and Egg Rock was a quiet place, affording him ample time to tend his traps; visit his sister, who was now living in the family home in Salem; and bet on his favorite ponies at the local track.

He also found time for the poems.

In the beginning, he decided to keep them locked up because, as Viola had confessed and he had seen for himself, they were unorthodox and disturbing, hardly the kind of material for a public library or, especially, the prying eyes of children. His jibe about pornography, which he had regretted as soon as the words were out of his mouth, wasn't so far off the mark after all.

In spite of himself, he kept bringing them out to have another look.

He typed out copies of each poem to protect the originals from damage. Since he was barely able to type, it became a laborious process of hunt and peck, but it allowed him to see inside each one for the first time. By the time he'd transcribed them all, he knew they would require hours and hours of study.

The number nine reminded him of novenas, nine-day devotions. Their popularity had declined, but when he was a child and during his seminary years, churches had held novenas, especially around Christmas and Easter. The faithful would fill churches for nine evenings running for prescribed prayers and petitions to God and, especially, the Virgin Mary for special graces.

The nine poems would serve as his nine prayers, one for each day of his private novena. With Ash Wednesday and Lent ahead, the timing couldn't have been better.

After setting the day's poem between two tall candles, he'd read it out loud, and after a period of silent reflection, he'd reread it silently before reading it out loud one last time. Then he'd carefully snuff the candles and sit in darkness, trying to discern just what the poem was telling him.

Candlelight, he felt, lent a solemnity to the proceedings. Midnight Mass on Christmas Eve, with the church bathed in the glow of scores of tapers, was his favorite ritual of the liturgical year.

In earlier years he'd refused to go anywhere near a lit candle. A near-fatal house fire in childhood had made him terrified of any open flame. The most difficult part of seminary—far harder than the courses on church history, scripture, and even Latin—had been getting over his fire phobia in the presence of lit candles at Mass.

He wept over the first poem, about love transcending time. It reminded him of a girl he'd known at fourteen, before religious life intruded.

He spent hours in the dark after reading the fifth night's poem, the most impertinent of them all. Line by line, step by step, the verses took aim at ritual, church, and, finally, God Himself in the poet's struggle to see the world "with clear-eyed honesty."

At dawn on the ninth day, he got a phone call from his priest friend at the chancery. The busybodies at the finance office had been reviewing Saint Lawrence's balance sheets for the umpteenth time, he reported. Their newly hired investigator was about to drive out to Egg Rock for a surprise visit.

"If you need to clean anything up," he added in a whisper, "you'd better get cracking."

It was a short walk from the back door of the rectory down the hill to the dock, and like most people, Father Ralph was a creature of habit. He'd celebrate Mass at seven, be in his boat by eight thirty, and have the traps pulled by nine. By then, the housekeeper would have the rectory in order, and he'd start the rest of his day.

Neighbors, mostly women clearing the breakfast dishes, waved from windows as he walked past. No one could tell that his backpack was heavier than usual.

The sea was so calm that he killed the motor and rowed, directing his dory to the spot where the water was deepest. After feathering the oars, he took a moment to steady his nerves. He looked back at the town, with the white steeple of Saint Lawrence's peeking over the trees, catching the morning sun. As he watched, the steeple began to waver, as if sitting atop a chimney on a winter day.

*An hour to get back,* he thought.

Instead of easing off, the shimmering filled his field of vision, obliterating everything else. Suddenly dizzy, he felt himself thrust backward over the side of the boat into the water.

The words *God's inscrutable ways* scrolled through his mind until the blackness took over.

The rectory housekeeper called the police when Father Ralph failed to return from tending his traps. Later in the day, an unmanned dory washed ashore at Forty Steps. The first officer on the scene radioed the station, noting that a lemon-colored packet resembling the one he'd reported missing from Miss Pettigrew's home back in December was sitting on the floor of the boat, tied to a brick.

# *W*AR TROPHIES

Whoever came up with the saying "Revenge is sweet" didn't have it quite right. Revenge delivers a buzz like any good drug. Intoxicating? You bet. Empowering? Yes, sir. Addicting? Oh yeah. Sweet? No way!

My story begins about forty years ago in Vietnam, where I spent two tours as an army medic. But I'll skip the Vietnam part for a moment while I fill you in on more recent stuff.

I've been living in Florida for a while. I saw an ad for cut-rate airfares in the papers, hopped on a flight, and never set foot in

Massachusetts again. My ex-wife, Karen, cleaned out my apartment in Egg Rock and sent my things down here once I got settled.

After Vietnam, I went to nursing school on the GI Bill, got my RN, and started as an OR nurse at a hospital in Boston. That was where I met Karen, a cute, bouncy, funny-as-hell lab technician. We started off trading jokes, but one thing led to another, and before I knew it, we were married, and Karen was pregnant. The day our baby, Flo, was born was the happiest day of my life. But just when life looked so full of hope, things took a bad turn. Flo's skin was slightly yellow when she arrived, but instead of having easy-to-treat neonatal jaundice, she had a blocked bile duct system and died of liver failure at three months of age.

Our marriage didn't survive either. Flo's death got in the way of everything, and we finally called it quits. The only positive news is that Karen and I have stayed on speaking terms ever since.

Those years after the divorce were a disaster. I drank like there was no tomorrow and began scoring recreational drugs behind the commuter rail station in Squimset. Looking back, I don't understand why it took me so long to realize that just about every substance I'd ever want was sitting right under my nose at the hospital. So I said goodbye to drug deals in sketchy neighborhoods and sleazy middlemen. No one at the hospital was the wiser while I siphoned off portions of the patients' opiate doses for my own use. Then I got sloppy, as all addicts do sooner or later.

The shift supervisor walked into an empty OR suite one morning and caught me standing under the bright lights, injecting a blockbuster dose of fentanyl into a leg vein.

Next came lawyers, courtrooms, jail time, rehab, rented rooms, halfway houses, menial jobs, unemployment, panhandling, and the realization that I couldn't get through more than a week of sobriety in all those years. Karen called it my slow-motion death spiral.

I survived this life on the margins for years before finally seeing the ad in the paper and flying south. It has paid off big-time. For whatever reason, I've been 100 percent clean and sober since that plane landed in West Coconut Beach five years ago.

I found a studio apartment in a gritty neighborhood just south of the airport. It was a far cry from sleepy Egg Rock, where a siren in the night is the talk of the town the next morning. My home in West Coconut has steel bars on the windows and double-bolted doors.

When gun shots ring out at night, a pretty common occurrence, I'm reminded of Vietnam.

But the ocean is only blocks away. If you've been brought up in a beach town like I was, you never want to be landlocked. I can't see the water from my place, but I can smell it when the wind is right.

Salt water is in my DNA, I guess. My mother once told me that her great-grandpa had been the Egg Rock lighthouse keeper. She tended to exaggerate, so I'm not sure if she was telling the truth.

Most people up north confuse West Coconut Beach with Coconut Beach, the barrier island just offshore. Although they are less than a mile apart and connected by a trio of bridges, West Coconut Beach and Coconut Beach might as well be in separate galaxies. CB is a playground for the rich, with zillion-dollar estates, Rolls-Royces at intersections, and celebrities vying for the best tables at five-star restaurants.

A drug conviction makes it hard to land a decent job, but I've been working for the same outfit since the first week I got here—as a bagger at a supermarket. Don't laugh. The work is steady, the benefits are generous, I have flexible hours, and I can ride my bike to work. For a people-watcher like me, it's the perfect perch. I'll always love the folks at Tropique Supermarkets because they gave me a chance when I needed it most.

I figured I was doing something right when they transferred me from the faded old Tropique in West Coconut Beach to their swank new supermarket out on the island.

The place is gorgeous. The parking spaces are separated by dwarf palms and bougainvillea, and when you enter the building through a Moorish colonnade, you could be in Granada. It's twice the size of my old store and must have been a marketing consultant's dream assignment. The shelves are packed with upscale goodies, which the good people of Coconut Beach pile into their supersized shopping carts.

If there's anything they don't stock, Tropique will gladly order it. One of the regulars, an eightyish lady who has an unmistakable German accent but claims to be from North Dakota, receives a weekly shipment of bratwurst and sauerkraut via a supplier in Dusseldorf.

None of my customers have asked me the obvious question: Why is a sixty-something guy standing there bagging groceries? Because they know I've reinvented myself just like they have.

Within days of starting in the new store, I bagged for a fellow who caught my eye. On the lapel of his polo shirt he wore a First Cav pin. The First Cav insignia is unmistakable, shaped like a bright yellow shield with a black line running across it diagonally from left to right and the silhouette of a horse's head in the upper right corner. Anybody who's seen one once can ID it at fifty feet the second time around.

The First Calvary Division was my old unit in Vietnam, and the customer made me wonder if our paths had ever crossed. He looked about my age, but nothing else about him rang a bell. Then again, what would after forty years? He certainly looked like he belonged in Coconut Beach, smartly dressed in white slacks and tasseled loafers with no socks. Only the First Cav pin and his buzz cut looked out of place, since Coconut Beach is not known as a military retirement community.

I kicked myself for looking at him so carefully. If I've learned one thing in my life, it's not to dwell too much on the war. That only complicates matters.

He asked me to wheel his groceries out to his vehicle. It's one of the perks offered by the new store, along with valet parking and shopping assistants.

"The car's over there, Larry," he said, having obviously read my name tag, "under that banyan tree, where it's nice and cool."

He was pointing at an emerald-colored Bentley sedan that looked as inviting as an oasis. The Florida plate displayed an unusual series of letters: FTFLNKR.

I helped him with the bags, and he slipped me a twenty, about twice the going tip. While I was pushing the cart back inside, the emerald oasis rolled by noiselessly, giving me another glimpse of the plate—and I had an epiphany. Fast Flanker was the radio handle for the battalion in which I'd spent a good chunk of my time.

I obsessed about the Cav pin and Fast Flanker for the rest of my shift, and when I got up to take a leak in the middle of the night, I realized I'd been dreaming about my old unit on the Cambodian border.

If Fast Flanker didn't return, I knew I could put the war back where it belonged. But it didn't work out that way.

A week later, just when I started to relax, the dude resurfaced.

"Good to be back," he said, giving me a clap on the shoulder.

From then on, he'd show up like clockwork every few days with that bright yellow First Cav pin attached to his crisp, carefully pressed shirt.

It got so obvious that Mabel, the clerk I usually partnered with, began referring to him as "Larry's new friend."

It got to be kind of a ritual. I'd bag the groceries and wheel them out to the Bentley, and he'd slip me a twenty.

As time went on, he got chatty.

"Ever served in the military, Larry?"

"No, sir, medical deferment."

Other times, he'd launch into how the military had changed his life, how it builds character, and so on, but he didn't ask any more personal questions.

One day, out of the blue, he introduced himself. I wanted to stick my fingers in my ears.

"Stan. Stan Rhodes."

We shook hands.

After work, I rode my bike out to the beach instead of going straight home. I was sitting on a bench at dusk, watching some die-hard surfers try for one last good wave, when it all clicked.

I was late in my second tour and officially a short-timer, with only days left in country. I'd been put in charge of our battalion aid station on a forward firebase after spending my first tour in the field. I really did run the place since the doctor, just out of an internship in California, spent day and night in his hooch, playing solitaire and writing letters home. Everybody called me Doc.

We always held extra sick call when a new company of troopers rotated in from the boonies.

That was when I first laid eyes on Staff Sergeant Stanley Rodowski. He herded a half dozen of his grunts into the waiting area and hung around until every one of them got checked out.

The first night in for a company always meant serious drinking, so I wasn't surprised to see the sergeant back in the aid station later on.

He wasn't sick, he said, but I could see that he was pretty wasted.

He'd come back because we had been good to his men, and he wanted to return the favor. He pulled an object from his backpack and motioned me to come close. It was one of the clear zip-lock bags used for combat rations, such as ready-to-eat spaghetti. Inside, floating in greenish liquid, was a human ear.

"A little war trophy. There are lots more where this baby came from. Name the anatomical part, Doc, and it's yours."

He sounded like a door-to-door salesman pitching encyclopedias.

Out came two more bags. In one floated a nose, and in the last was a plump, spidery thing. He lifted it closer to the lightbulb hanging from the ceiling.

It was a baby's hand.

It had been severed at the wrist, and as he rocked it back and forth, a remnant of tissue trailed behind like a streamer attached to a kite on a breezy day. The fingers were half clenched, as if it once held a toy or was about to throw a ball. Mother-of-pearl fingernails reflected the light.

I made it outside just in time to barf up my supper.

By the time I returned, Staff Sergeant Rodowski had taken off. The next morning, I watched him and the rest of his unit climb into choppers heading back to the boonies, and soon after that, I boarded a Freedom Bird bound for the States and the rest of my life.

---

I was still sitting on the beach, watching the stars come out, when I hit on a plan.

From what I could see, Fast Flanker was a man of steady habits. At the Tropique, he bought pretty much the same stuff. Two items he never failed to pick up were a large bottle of California estate cabernet ($189.99) and a two-ounce bag of cognac-infused chocolates ($24.50). On one of our trips to the parking lot, he explained.

"You see, Larry, I've had a couple of heart attacks, and my cardiologist isn't making any promises. No sex. No exertion. No stress. Doctor's orders. Wine and chocolate are my only indulgences these days. After feasting on them, I take a lazy dip in my pool. Heaven on earth!"

I might be a little behind the times, but I know for a fact that some of the old remedies work just fine today. I ordered the digitalis capsules online, brought a bag of Fast Flanker's favorite chocolates home, and went to work. It felt like the good old days, handling a syringe. Only this time, I was injecting chocolate candies instead of my surgical patients or myself.

Digitalis has been around for centuries and was still widely prescribed when I was in nursing. Nowadays there are newer medications, but dig (rhymes with fridge) is still out there. One reason it's not used so much is its toxicity. With too heavy a dose, even a normal heart blocks down and fires off crazy premature beats that lead to ventricular fibrillation—until your ticker finally goes flat line. With Fast Flanker's history, no one would be the wiser if his heart gave out. Besides, I couldn't imagine anybody running a tox screen on Stan Rhodes's candy supply.

The next time Fast Flanker showed up, I simply switched the bags of chocolates while he was swiping his platinum card for Mabel.

Mabel waved a copy of the *Coconut Beach Clarion* in front of me when I got into work later that week. "Larry, look at this! Your buddy kicked the bucket."

Fast Flanker had made the front page with the headline "Noted Financier's Body Found in Pool." An accompanying photo showed him in a tux with the First Cav pin on the lapel.

"There go my tips, Mabel."

During break, I devoured the story. A maid had found the body. Stan Rhodes had been known to have a medical condition, and according to the police, the death did not appear suspicious.

The rest of the article was short on facts. He'd been a "highly successful venture capitalist and entrepreneur in the biomedical field" who'd spent most of his professional life in Asia. He left no immediate survivors, and a memorial service was planned for a later date.

It's been a while since Fast Flanker's passing. I might look like the same unassuming guy, bagging groceries and making small talk with my customers, but I'm still flying. I worry that I'm coming off the high, though. I have no plans yet, but every day I encounter folks whose absence would make the world a better place, and you know, a quick and painless arrhythmia isn't a half bad way to check out.

One other thing: Karen and I have been emailing a lot and started talking on the phone. We're back to joking just like we did in those first wonderful months together. You see, I never stopped loving her. I was even able to tell her about my recurring dream. I'm in the neonatal ICU. Flo wraps her tiny fingers around my pinkie and won't let go.

Karen seems happy that I'm finally opening up and has made a reservation to fly down for a visit.

We've also been talking about my coming home. I expected to stay here for keeps, but with Karen back in the picture, I'm getting homesick. In her last email, she attached a snapshot of the two of us at Forty Steps, reminding me that Egg Rock is still my favorite place on the planet.

What if I crave another buzz? No problem. There are plenty of folks from the old hometown whose demise would make this world a better place.

No problem at all.

# $S$EISMIC EVENTS

My name is Vincent. I was named after my great-great-uncle. Actually, Vincent isn't my official name anymore. I'll explain why later on.

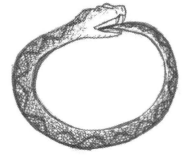

The name means "Conqueror," suggesting violence, but I'm a peaceful man. The only thing I've conquered in my long life is time.

Like any youngster, I never gave growing old more than a passing thought, and I never imagined I'd become the sole survivor of a generation. I can't be entirely sure that I'm the oldest person in the United Christian Commonwealth, known as the UCC, now that we have only the most primitive modes of communication left. The most I can say is that I haven't heard about anyone from the world I grew up in for a long time.

Egg Rock was full of eighty-year-olds when I was a kid. Now I seem to be the last leaf on the tree.

People die young now. It's as if we're living in medieval times all over again.

At first, the biggest killer was bluboy disease, named after a cartoon character popular more than a century ago. How a cute little guy in a cartoon came to represent such a dreaded disease is bizarre, but that's what happened.

Bluboy disease hit my mother and father the same summer, when they were both in their fifties. My wife and son were also victims, in their thirties. They were all textbook cases: healthy people who noticed a painless bright blue blemish that spread over every millimeter of their skin in a matter of days. At the end, they coughed up gobs of blue phlegm and suffocated.

Once the government decided that bluboy disease was caused by ultraviolet rays, the authorities handed out giant tubes of ointment. People who didn't apply it to all sun-exposed skin were sent to camps in what was once called the state of Maine, but the ointment did nothing more than stain our clothes.

Unfortunately, bluboy disease was only the beginning.

The first things to disappear after the government broke down were medications. Pharmacies closed for lack of inventory, and lifesavers, such as antibiotics, vaccines, and even anesthetics used in surgery, became available only on the black market—at astronomical prices. Inevitably, diseases long thought eradicated reappeared.

Cosmas, my grandson and only living relative, lost his twin brother to tetanus when they were fifteen. Damian stepped on a nail, and before we knew it, he got sick. It's hard to imagine, but tetanus is even more gruesome than bluboy. Before he died, Damian's face tensed up, his eyes bulged as if they'd explode out of their sockets, and his lips retracted, giving him a hideous smile.

Soon after we buried Damian, the plague appeared. That was when I felt we'd time-traveled back to Europe in the 1300s.

Just about everyone died. I expected wholesale anarchy, but the would-be anarchists must have been killed off along with everybody else. These days, we few survivors are scattered about the area, too busy trying to stay alive to fight about anything.

What you are reading, whoever you might be, is a brief history. When I'm gone, there won't be anyone left to explain who we are and where we come from. I was a history teacher in the days before what was once called New England seceded from the former United States. I often feel I was spared in order to bear witness.

History was outlawed after the Secession, as if the past never existed. Books were confiscated, teachers (like me) were fired, and even writing was prohibited. The mere possession of writing materials meant an automatic prison sentence, but I took a chance and hid pens, paper, and even an ancient typewriter in case I ever got the chance to be a historian again.

Our clan has been living on Sagamore Hill in what used to be called Squimset, Massachusetts, since 2050. For generations before that, we lived in Egg Rock, a pair of small islands just offshore. Our house was in the lowest part of Egg Rock, on the northwestern tip of the larger island.

F. X. Mulcahy settled in Egg Rock nearly two hundred years ago. Fresh off the boat, he fell in love with the rocky shore north of Boston because it reminded him of his native Galway. He started working as a fisherman and soon got into the lobster business. He was successful enough to build the family home on the island, where, five generations later, I grew up.

I was still a college student when a violent nor'easter struck Egg Rock. The storm surge tore into Squimset Bay and put our property underwater for weeks.

No one in Egg Rock got hit harder than we did.

Townspeople repaired the damage and hung on. Talk of global warming, so common thirty years earlier, had long been considered unpatriotic, so when the storm brought a king tide to Egg Rock, the news reports assured us that it was a once-in-a-century event.

My father called a family meeting to discuss the situation. He believed Egg Rock was doomed, but he couldn't bear the thought of moving away without all of us agreeing to do so. Only when every one raised a hand in favor of abandoning Egg Rock did he let us in on his plan.

A house on the top of Sagamore Hill was about to go on the market. It was a house my father knew well since his best friend from childhood had lived there. He made an offer right away.

He was worried the Egg Rock property would never sell, but

buyers with real money lined up. Sitting on its private point of land with killer views in all directions, the Mulcahy house was seductive—a femme fatale, my father called it.

We moved everything we could carry to Sagamore Hill in record time, all the while worrying that another storm would strike, flood us all over again, and ruin the deal.

Actually, Egg Rock hung on for another twenty-five fretful years. The lowlands where our house stood and most of the golf course around Bear Pond disappeared long before the end, and eventually, the causeway was underwater for twenty-two hours a day. The end came swiftly. A series of storms in the fall of 2075—year 25 in the New Calendar—caused the worst flooding in memory, and the water never receded after that. The last of the holdouts piled everything they could into boats and fled to higher ground.

Egg Rock wasn't alone. Farther south, Nantucket, Martha's Vineyard, and most of Cape Cod were lost. Boston soldiered on with dikes and high-powered pumps, while its downtown streets were converted to canals. One mayor touted Boston as the new Venice as it lost block after block to the tides and finally ceased to exist.

The capital of the UCC was moved from its original location in Plymouth to the slopes of Mount Tabor, formerly known as Mount Monadnock, in what was once the state of New Hampshire.

Sagamore Hill was a comfortable hundred feet above sea level and was close enough to Egg Rock to create the illusion that we'd never left. Like Egg Rock, the hill had a colorful history. Winnipurket, the sachem of the Naumkeag tribe, was thought to have lived there when the first Europeans arrived nearly five hundred years ago.

Soon after moving, I made a discovery that allowed our family to hang on through the Secession, the Lawless Period, and the Great Plague that lay ahead. While planting a vegetable garden behind the house, I stumbled onto the entrance to a small cave. Since I had a premonition that even worse times were coming, we quietly extended it with a network of tunnels.

I got the idea for the tunnels from a memoir written by my great-grandfather Leo Mulcahy. He'd been an army medic in one of those long-forgotten twentieth-century wars, during which the enemy hid in elaborate tunnels and remained undetected for years. Leo had a full and interesting life, but it was cut short when he was poisoned by a nurse from a hospital where he had once worked.

The nurse turned out to be a notorious serial killer, and Leo was his final victim.

We excavated the tunnels during tumultuous times. Washington flooded and the federal capital was moved west to Denver. Coastal cities all over the world, including Tokyo, Shanghai, Sydney, Athens, London, and New York, were all abandoned.

The Vatican was destroyed by a dirty bomb, and Rome, already flooding, was evacuated because of radiation. Soon the entire Mediterranean basin was inundated. Whole cities relocated to the mountains and were fortified with walls and guard towers to defend against hordes of refugees.

At that point, the United States closed all borders and held its last election, voting for a president who declared martial law, dismissed Congress, and declared the courts unconstitutional.

New England seceded from the United States the same year that Egg Rock was abandoned, and overnight, the region was renamed the United Christian Commonwealth. By the end of the next year, all non-Christians had been deported, and a tall electrified fence had been erected all the way from the former state of Connecticut to the border of what was once called Canada.

The man known only as the Patriarch is the supreme leader of the UCC. In the early years, he appeared on television, blessing crowds and dedicating buildings. People assume he's still the Patriarch, but no one knows for sure.

The Language Modernization Act became law at that time. It forbade the speaking, writing, reading, and teaching of all foreign languages; outlawed all books and studies deemed nonessential; and restructured the educational system. Vocational and theological studies were permitted, but little else was.

I became a janitor in the same school where I had taught history.

The New Rules meant that the names of all newborns were to come from an approved list of saints, and people who happened to have unapproved names, as I did, were encouraged to change them. Days of the week and months of the year were replaced by saints' and prophets' names. May, the easiest, became Mary, and Thursday, for instance, became Jeremiah.

On Abstinence Daniels and Hoseas (Tuesdays and Fridays) consumption of meat was prohibited. On the Sabbath, religious services were mandatory, and fasting was strongly encouraged.

The old calendar was outlawed, and the year 2051 officially became year 1.

Fancy clothing was frowned upon, as were jewelry, bright colors, and obvious signs of ostentation. The Patriarch always appeared in black.

However, an underground hummed along out of sight. People only used official names when the religious police were snooping around, and barely anybody fully complied with the rules for fasting and abstinence. No one I knew used the New Calendar in private. People read so-called nonessential books surreptitiously. There never was a book burning, although I was convinced that a National Bonfire Day was only a matter of time.

As time went on, I moved the old Egg Rock family library into the tunnels. A librarian ancestor had collected books, papers, diaries, pictures, and computer records of the family more than a hundred years ago. By the time I was born, her original collection had doubled in size.

Cosmas is fascinated by the stuff I dragged into the tunnels, calling it our family museum. I filled one chamber with appliances and electronics, all useless without electricity. As a child, he'd fiddle with the TV remote, imagining a picture appearing on the empty flat screen affixed to a wall. I repurposed two large refrigerators and a freezer to keep the most valuable books, documents, and pictures safe. An old stove and a couple of microwaves also became secure storage spaces. Computers and cell phones sit silently, gathering dust, waiting for power to return. Cosmas's favorite object, however, doesn't require electricity to function. It's an ancient Remington typewriter once owned by my great-great-great-grandfather, F. X. Mulcahy. Cosmas still loves to run his fingers over the ends of the keys, feeling the contour of the characters. But without an ink ribbon, it can't produce a single legible letter.

Everything I write now is in pencil since the pens I'd hidden away have all dried up.

The Lawless Period and the Great Plague, two periods that overlapped when the UCC was barely twenty years old, spelled the end of the New Rules.

During the Lawless Period, there was widespread civil unrest, with looting, kidnapping, and burning of churches and homes. Pirates anchored offshore and attacked seaside towns, including Squimset.

The Lawless Period gave way to the most horrific period of

my life, the Great Plague. From April to November of 2107 (from Esther to Ruth in year 57), more than 99 percent of the population was wiped out. The illness came on quickly, leading to high fever, leopard spots (black sores on the head and neck), shock, and death within twelve hours. The two of us cowered in the tunnels while gangs overran our property inches above our heads.

The plague, like the fourteenth-century version, was spread by rats and their fleas.

I'd discovered rats getting into our food and gnawing on books back when I'd started building the tunnels. Rat poison spread around the tunnel entrances and air ducts eliminated the problem, so I stocked up. When the plague broke out, we were the only ones who were prepared. Without that piece of good luck, the rats and their fleas would have overwhelmed us too.

When we finally emerged, the world we had known was gone.

The gangs, pirates, and religious police had all vanished. The only sounds came from the wind in the trees and the caws of seagulls.

The devastation was unimaginable. All the buildings on Sagamore Hill had been destroyed, and there was no sign that any of our neighbors had made it. Scanning all quadrants through my binoculars, I saw no signs of life.

The nights were darker than I'd thought possible. I kept looking for a campfire or other sign of humanity, but there was nothing.

The tunnels had saved us—and preserved our history. My father, so proud of his Irish heritage, once had compared us to the Irish monks who preserved the classical and religious writings of Western civilization in their manuscripts and hid them from pillagers during the Dark Ages.

One night, Cosmas turned to me with tears in his eyes. "What if we're the only ones left?"

"Impossible," I answered with as much conviction as I could summon.

We weren't alone after all. One day a stranger with a long beard and hair down to his shoulders appeared at the top of the hill. I raised my rifle in warning.

"Vincent, put that thing down!"

Michael, the only other teacher at my school to graduate to janitorial duty, gave me an embrace, and when Cosmas joined us, the three of us danced around like children.

He had hiked over from a town several miles inland, where he and about a dozen other survivors had barricaded themselves in an abandoned police station.

He had once visited the tunnels and made the trip to Sagamore Hill in hopes we'd survived.

Michael has been back, of course, and soon others appeared from time to time, reassuring us that we're not entirely on our own.

It's been sixty years since we abandoned Egg Rock, but Cosmas and I still get out there from time to time on our boat. He loves to listen to stories about the place and knows many by heart. His favorite, the one he asks me to tell every time we row out there, is about how Bear Pond got its name.

Each time we go, I say a prayer for my ancestors who are buried there. When he's in the mood, Cosmas joins in.

These days, fishing season runs from November to April. During the rest of the year, the sun is too dangerous. During the long summer days, we stay underground and venture outside only at night. The ocean is more perilous in the summer too. Giant Portuguese man-o'-war, unheard of in Egg Rock when I was a kid, cover the surface of bays and inlets, each one packing enough venom to kill a two-hundred-pound man. Manatees are another import from the tropics. Once known as the gentlest of marine creatures, they have learned to overturn boats and attack their occupants. Cod have been wiped out by overfishing and rising ocean temperatures, but like the man-o'-war and the manatees, other fish have moved north to fill the vacuum. Red snappers are my favorite new fish, but alas, they are rare finds, a cause for celebration. The most common catch these days is the saltwater pigfish, which is only a few inches long but easy to identify by its orange spots and stripes. They are an acquired taste, but with persistence, I've become a connoisseur.

Many fish are deformed, with one eye, two heads, and so on, but we only eat the mutants when there is no choice.

Now, thanks to Michael, we're in contact with a few other small settlements nearby, where there's a market for fresh fish. Money is a thing of the past, but we trade our fish for their meat and vegetables, and everyone is happy.

However, if money ever returns, my descendants will be well provided for. My stash of 24-carat gold Uncle Sams, minted shortly before Washington went underwater, awaits them, buried in the deepest tunnel.

On our first fishing trip of the season, I asked Cosmas to row out to Egg Rock. Good hauls can be had nearer home, but he knows how much I loved the place, so he agreed to make the trip.

At low tide, a few remnants of the old town come close to the water's surface, but that day's tides coincided with a full moon, giving us a chance of seeing more of the town than usual.

We anchored over what used to be called East Point, where the top of one old house pokes through the surface at the lowest tides. It was built back when well-to-do families from Boston spent the summer in huge buildings that they, with tongue firmly in cheek, called cottages.

This old cottage was called Whitecaps. When I was a child, it was still occupied, and I recall being fascinated by what looked like a balcony attached to the roof. My mother called it a widow's walk, so named because a sea captain's wife would wait there, sometimes in vain, for her husband to return.

The widow's walk broke through the surface minutes after we anchored, followed by the entire roof line. I hadn't seen so much of Egg Rock in years.

Just then, our boat started bobbing like a bathtub toy, and the house began to shake. Cosmas and I rowed away as hard as we could, and when I looked back, the house had completely risen out of the ocean. Then it flew apart with a crash, as if a giant had chopped through it with the back of his hand.

Earthquakes, unheard of when I was young, have become common. Usually, they do little more than knock objects off tables or crack mirrors, but this one was a different order of magnitude. A rumbling sound went on for several minutes while Whitecaps came apart, scattering debris on the now exposed hill where it had stood for so long. In the distance, I could make out the silhouette of another hill, where an old veterans' club once existed. Cosmas turned and pointed out Castle Rock rising out of the water, near a beach we had once called Forty Steps.

When I suggested we have a closer look, he fixed his piercing blue eyes on me and dug his oars in.

The giant rock formation glinted in sunlight for the first time in decades. The surface was wildly irregular, with innumerable outcroppings and crevices. It reminded me of a castle that had once appeared to me in a crazy dream.

Sitting inches above the water line, inside a deep crevice, sat a nearly translucent white boulder. It looked so out of place that it could have dropped out of the sky.

Without a word between us, we dumped our haul of fish and eased the boulder into the middle of the boat. The hull sunk so deep into the water that we nearly swamped, but just as the ocean was about to pour over the gunwales, the rowboat righted itself.

Etched on the stone was the image of a bearded man holding a hammer in one hand and a lightning bolt in the other, encircled by a serpent biting its tail.

We rowed back to Sagamore Hill with great care, afraid we'd capsize any second. I imagined the two of us pitching overboard and our treasure ending up at the bottom of Egg Rock Bay.

Much of Egg Rock was visible again, as was the rock itself, crouched like a watchdog astern. It brought to mind an old postcard in my collection that shows the rock topped by a granite lighthouse two hundred years ago. We hugged the newly revealed shoreline on our way home, passing the Black Mine and John's Peril, places I hadn't thought about in years.

Now we can see Egg Rock from Sagamore Hill every day. It looks almost the way it did before it finally flooded out. Even the old causeway linking Egg Rock's two islands to the mainland breaks the surface of the water for an hour or so at each low tide.

In the weeks since the earthquake, people have been showing up at Sagamore Hill after hearing rumors about the mysterious white stone. More and more trickle in all the time. Some arrive on horseback, like the Canterbury pilgrims.

They bring flowers, prayers, and gifts as they pass through.

Some linger as if in a trance. A beautiful young pilgrim named Claudia has stayed on and has become Cosmas's friend.

Cosmas is as industrious as ever, bringing in hauls of fish and working our vegetable garden, but the nearly translucent white stone is never far from his mind. I told him everything I know about rune stones and was able to show him some pictures in an old history book from our underground library.

How this stone ended up in a crevice at Castle Rock is a mystery. It seems to validate the legend of the Vikings exploring Egg Rock, but there have been many hoax artifacts of the Norse exploration, so I'm keeping an open mind.

We keep the stone safe inside the tunnels. One pilgrim at a time is allowed to visit but only after being thoroughly frisked. I have volunteered to sit with the stone, and the more I contemplate it, the more I feel a sense of peace.

Back in my teaching days, I pictured history as a linear process, flowing like a river, but if the last few years have taught me anything, it's that instead of moving forward, history turns on itself.

At times, the clock runs backward.

Perhaps the Viking explorers left the stone, with its encircling serpent, as a reminder that history is merely a reflection of the cycles of day and night, the seasons, and birth and death. That's how I like to think of such things now.

Cosmas is too pragmatic to waste time worrying about the flow of history. He's convinced we were picked to survive the Lawless Period and the Great Plague, destined to visit Egg Rock during the earthquake, and selected to discover what he calls the "sacred stone."

He speaks of a new religion based on this narrative. He's making plans for an ornate tabernacle to house the stone and now appears dressed head to toe in black.

Cosmas and Claudia sat me down this morning to tell me that their baby, my great-grandchild, will arrive in the fall.

I only hope I can hold out until then. On the day I hold the newborn in my arms, I'll know I did my best to keep the cycle of life going—and I'll be able to rest at last.

# ABOUT THE AUTHOR

Terrence Murphy was born in Salem and brought up in Nahant, Massachusetts. He is a graduate of Phillips Exeter Academy, Harvard College, and the University of Virginia School of Medicine. He and his wife, Betty Wood, practiced medicine in Brookline and Brighton, Massachusetts, and currently live in Chestnut Hill, just outside of Boston. They have two children and four grandchildren.

His novel *Assumption City* was published in 2012.